The Perfect Front

The Perfect Front

Authored by
LaDawna S. Byers

(former student of A.J. [Donnell?] [North Parkway?] (Middle))

iUniverse, Inc.
New York Lincoln Shanghai

The Perfect Front

Copyright © 2006 by LaDawna S. Byers

All rights reserved. No part of this book may be used or reproduced by any means, graphic, electronic, or mechanical, including photocopying, recording, taping or by any information storage retrieval system without the written permission of the publisher except in the case of brief quotations embodied in critical articles and reviews.

iUniverse books may be ordered through booksellers or by contacting:

iUniverse
2021 Pine Lake Road, Suite 100
Lincoln, NE 68512
www.iuniverse.com
1-800-Authors (1-800-288-4677)

This is a work of fiction. All of the characters, names, incidents, organizations and dialogue in this novel are either the products of the author's imagination or are used fictitiously.

ISBN-13: 978-0-595-40438-4 (pbk)
ISBN-13: 978-0-595-84813-3 (ebk)
ISBN-10: 0-595-40438-3 (pbk)
ISBN-10: 0-595-84813-3 (ebk)

Printed in the United States of America

Acknowledgements

As I sat and tried to think of the things that I wanted to say in my acknowledgments, I realized that writing this part is far more difficult than writing the actual book. There are so many people that come to mind when I think of the word "acknowledge". If I miss anyone, please fault my mind and not my heart.

First of all, I want to PRAISE GOD for this opportunity. Lord, I thank you for the gift of expression and the sense of peace that you have given me throughout this entire process. You have held onto me through the years and protected me when I was too foolish to realize that I needed protecting and Lord, I thank you. You have given me a wonderfully supportive family, and blessed me far beyond what I deserve and to you I give all the praise. I pray that someone finds a blessing in this book and discovers the joy that lies in you.

Next, I want to say thank you to my other half. Buck, you have supported me through this whole crazy creative process. You pushed me through the writer's block, pulled me through the slumps, and held the kids down when I needed to "think". With you on my team I know this is just the beginning. I love you!

Next to all my babies—Lil' Mario, Justin, Taelor, and JJ, I love ya'll. I want to make you all proud. I couldn't have asked for better children—you are all true blessings. Mama, Daddy, Brian, and Michael thank you all for seeing to it that I had a fighting chance in this world. I was a crazy kid and you never gave up on me.

To those of you who gave me advice, believed in me, and supported me I want to say thank you so much. Special thanks to: Gail, Kendrah, Yolanda, Mrs. Cain, Teresa, Gwen, Jameika, Katrena, Shasta, LaRhonda, Tsutae, Lisa, and Chantel. All of you did a little something to help me along the way.

In closing I would like to thank each and everyone one of you who are taking the time to pick up this book and share in my dream. I appreciate you all and I hope to share more thoughts with you as God sees fit to bless me with them.

Thanks,

LaDawna S. Byers

Introduction

The rain came down in a mist, seeming almost weightless. A thick fog clung to all four windows with the tiny handprints of my children scattered throughout. The sky looked as if God had dipped his brush in black and splattered it on top of darkness. I sat outside of Jalen's office in an unlit parking lot covered in gloom that seemed to swallow me whole. Slowly, I held my hand up in front of my face and saw nothing. Aside from the tingling sensation that the winter cold brought to my fingertips, there was no feeling within my physical body. I watched as drops of water accumulated in little puddles on the glass until they ran over and down the windshield. Beads of water accumulated in my eyes until they too became too heavy with my burdens and ran down my cheeks. The intensity grew and I gripped the gun tightly in my right hand battling the urge to pull the trigger. It felt smooth and cool; final yet right. At that exact moment I held redemption, well some twisted form of it I guess.

Fear caused my hand to shake as I waited on something to snap me back into reality and convince me to put the gun down and drive back to my warm home, and my beautiful children. Projections of my life ran silently through my mind in bright flashes. Slide after slide went by, each representing crucial moments in my development, marriage, and self-destruction. Eyes closed, I extended my hands straight out and my head began to spin just as it had when my absent daddy would swing me in circles as a little girl.

I pictured Kylen and Kaylen's first Christmas together. That morning the house smelled of warm cinnamon with a hint of pine from the freshly cut Christmas tree. Suddenly, a cold sweat came over me as the picture switched to my babies living their lives without their mother. Years earlier as a young lady, I buried my mother and had managed to screw my life up quickly in her absence. Taking a moment, I began to think about my funeral—what would be said and who would attend? On the front pew only feet away from my remains, I pictured Jalen's face and wondered if this drastic step would finally pull remorse into his mind.

What had my life represented up until now? Questions flooded my mind, waiting for my heart to provide the summary of my obituary. What would my children think of me? Would suicide mean certain hell? Could this pain that I had carried for years ever be healed? Death was so permanent, yet nothing inside of me made me wanted to hold on to this life. The suffering was unbearable and my life had lost all value. I existed only as a mother to my children, a doormat to my ex-husband, and a step-mother to a couple of shameful secrets.

The songs on the radio had been solemn that night adding more despair to my current state of mind. The lyrics of *Bohemian Rhapsody* seemed to cry with me and the words were reaffirming my feelings of guilt, hatred, and weariness. "Mama life has just begun; but now I've gone and thrown it all away. I don't wanna die—but I sometimes wish I'd never been born at all", the velvet smooth voice sang what I too felt in my heart. I related fully to the song and felt that maybe it was time to be through with this world—because the world was definitely through with me.

I placed the gun safely in my lap as I thought about the events that had pushed me to this point. Laying my head back on the headrest, I allowed my mind to retrace the painful events that led me here. For me, life started on what was truly the most beautiful day of my life...

Chapter 1

I held my breath as I waited on his answer, "I do," he said with eyes as sure as yesterday. I knew that would be his answer but still the seconds that it took for it to leave his lips were like an eternity. Victor leaned in and handed Jalen the ring and he slipped it on my finger ever so gently. As he did, it sparkled ever so brilliantly, as only 10 doctor's paychecks in one ring could. I slipped his wedding band on his finger, looking him right in the eyes. I could look there forever but we had a ceremony to finish. The rest of the preacher's words were a blur, I wasn't listening to him or anything else that he said. I was waiting to hear for the first time, Mr. and Mrs. Jalen Starks—that would seal the deal. The church erupted in cheers as the baritone voice of the preacher announced us as husband and wife for the very first time. I was stunned, ecstatic, and proud to hear it. I turned and faced the guests as a brand new woman. There were at least 300 people gazing at me and enjoying this very beautiful occasion. The man I loved held my hand, grinned proudly, and presented me as his wife to the group.

As my groom and I exited the church, I felt a very eerie feeling come over me. The beauty of the day was picturesque. I nervously ran my hands over my absolutely stunning Princess White gown. The pearl beaded bodice enhanced and played up every single curve I had. My husband stood next to me in a white tuxedo that was tailored specifically for him. It fit him as naturally as his own skin. He looked amazing and so did I—yet I still felt uneasiness in my stomach that caused it to knot up.

As we entered the reception the lights were dim in a room filled with flickering candles of all sizes reflecting through crystal centerpieces. The shadows of the flames dancing on the wall added to the magic in the air. With my train trailing what seemed like miles behind, Jalen spun me into his arms and held me there. "If this World Were Mine" floated through the air and encircled my husband and me as we shared a marital kiss. He whispered the words to the song in my ear as we danced and time stopped in this room that was empty for the moment. It seemed to be only Jalen, me, and one more set of eyes, watching us attentively. They were eyes that I knew from somewhere but had never actually met anywhere. As the song grew louder, Jalen held me closer and the breath from his words on my neck made even the last remaining person in the room fade into the background of my husband and our first dance.

There was a thunderous applause that snapped me back to the reality of my reception. Jalen kissed me once more and escorted me hand in hand to the head table where our wedding attendants waited. At the table sat Kaiya, my maid of honor; Victor, the best man; Ivy and Chelle, the bridesmaids; and Curtis and Tyler, the groomsmen. One could say that we represented the Elite of Virginia. Our table consisted of lawyers, doctors, entrepreneurs, athletes, and actors. They all stood and greeted us, obviously proud of our commitment. They later gave intimate toasts of heartfelt congratulations and well-wishes.

Dinner was exquisite and as we began to mingle with the guests, I longed to have some family to be there, and to share in my happiness with me. I received over 400 people in what was intended to be only a 300-person reception. As I bit down on the last strawberry on my plate, I noticed the strange eyes were now set on my husband as he visited with guests across the room. His eyes subtly returned the favor. They were not affectionate glances but rather familiar acknowledgments. Just as suspicion arose within me, Kaiya came over—smoothed my hair down and plopped down in the seat next to me.

"Girl my feet really hurt! You just had to pick the five inch heels for us! I don't know how I am going to make it through the pictures that we have left to take. Where is Jalen? I am about to finish his shrimp because it's all gone at the serving table. Ya'll cheap butts didn't even get enough food."

Kaiya went from subject to subject before I had time to speak on anything. "Ky, get out of his plate, and why are you over here any way? Where is Mark? You better find him before that woman who pushed everyone down to get the bouquet gets to him. Who was she anyway? She has been staring at me and Jalen the whole evening. She must be one of his guests. Get up. Here comes my new husband now-".

Jalen sat down next to me; his cologne drifted under my nose and captivated my sense. He was so sophisticated, so sexy, and all mine. He leaned over and kissed me tenderly saying, "I missed you already," I allowed the kiss to hit my cheek and reminded him that after tonight he would not be out of my sight for at least a week in Maui. We both grinned at the thought of our upcoming honeymoon. It would be my very first time and his first with me—we were going to share something completely new and sacred.

"Congratulations! I never thought Jalen would get married—considering who he used to be." The moment between my husband and I was interrupted almost rudely by the young lady that seemed to bother me all night long. She stood in front of us in a stand-offish stance with her hand on her hip and her pinky finger in the corner of her pouty mouth. Her chestnut eyes looked directly at Jalen as she spoke. She had long silky tresses ironed bone straight and slightly tinted. The dress she wore left nothing to the imagination. Irritated by her presence, I noticed that she also was wearing white-of all colors. She was tall with wide hips and a small waist. Her stomach was flat for the most part, give or take a few womanly pounds in her midsection. The French manicure on her neat nails was soft and classic.

Her nervousness showed in the way she tightly clutched her designer handbag and tapped her left toe in shoes that complimented her purse nicely—clashing with her nasty attitude.

Breaking the concentration between the two of them I laughed off her comment and replied, "Thanks! Honey, Jalen's playin' in the past was his way of practicing while he waited for the right one to come along! Now he is ready for our future—aren't you babe!" I kissed my husband and he responded lovingly by kissing me back and stated, "You know what they say. Practice makes perfect." He kissed me again and when our lips finally parted—the young lady was gone. I watched her prance off with a deliberate sway in her hips that screamed "look at me".

"Jalen—who is she? Why is she here?"

He looked at me surprisingly, hunched his shoulders and said, "I don't know—ask her. All I know is she was a patient of mine that came in one time and never came back. I have seen her around a couple of times but that's it. I thought you knew her. Baby, did you eat my shrimp? I know I had some shrimp on my plate before I left."

"Ky ate your shrimp," I answered quickly and got back to the subject. "I didn't invite her so who did?"

"We didn't invite most of the people here; they just heard about it—knew us—knew there would be free food and came—you know how folks can be. Baby, let it go—this is our night." Jalen sounded irritated and rightfully so. It was my wedding day, and I had been saving myself for this experience. Jalen paid a great deal of money for me to have a dream day and I decided at that moment that I was overreacting to this girl. She could crash my wedding but she couldn't ruin my day. I leaned on my husband as I hugged him and let the music carry me right into the evening.

Maui was beautiful; the sky seemed to open up as we lay on the beach and enjoyed the company of each other. The mood between us was open and sensual; I truly enjoyed my husband. He made me "his" this week—opening the one gift that I had never given to anyone else.

As we lay on the beach, he showed me his appreciation in the way he looked at me, the way he held me, and the way he smiled at me for no reason whatsoever. Breaking the very comfortable silence between us, I whispered, "Can you believe that I am Mrs. Dr. Jalen Starks, M.D? How does that sound to you hon?"

"That's hot," he replied, "like music to my ears. Baby let's go inside the condo, we can look at the beach from there."

He grabbed me by my waist and led me inside—I knew the last thing he wanted to do inside was watch the beach. He wanted to play with his new toy some more and I most definitely wanted the same thing. There was a romantic connection between my husband and me.

I awoke to the breeze that came off of the ocean and into our window. We had a beach side condo that allowed us to enjoy the gentle sounds of the ocean. I rolled over and noticed that Jalen wasn't next to me. Lazily, I walked to the kitchen, sat on the cabinet, and sipped from a glass of flat champagne from the night before. As I drank, I heard quiet arguing from the bathroom; Jalen was on the phone having what seemed to be a very heated conversation. The volume of his cell phone was high, allowing me to hear a muffled female voice. I listened attentively from the outside door, however the walls hushed the words and I could not make out the subject matter of the conversation. After a few more moments of strained sadly ineffective spying, curiosity got the best of me. I got up slowly and walked towards the bathroom door.

Just as I reached for the knob, the conversation met a sudden end, and the bathroom door creaked opened. My husband emerged clearly frustrated, looking down at his feet. Only after taking a few steps did Jalen notice that I was standing there with two fresh glasses of champagne in my hands. He looked up, and the expression on his face quickly changed to delight.

"My princess has awaken, is that for me-thanks baby!" Jalen spoke as he ran his fingers through my hair, down my back, and around my waist. "Can we drink this from the patio?"

"Sure, baby who was that and why were you fussing on the phone? Am I going to have to curse someone out for upsetting my husband on our honeymoon?"

"No baby, it's just the office. Apparently they scheduled a few appointments for this week and one of my biggest clients and patients is demanding to see me day after tomorrow. I don't want to lose their business, but it is our honeymoon so I refuse to upset you."

As he spoke, I could tell that this conversation would come up again before the day was out. I mentally began packing my bags—sure that my workaholic husband would be ready to head home early. Wearing only a smile, I sat softly on the bed and extended my glass to meet my husband's as we toasted to "us forever".

Chapter 2

Steam covered the bathroom mirror, distorting my reflection. Using my bath towel, I wiped it from the mirror in an effort to distract my mind from the results of the test that sat on the counter. My hair was still wet from the shower; I combed through it and tried not to bother the test that sat there holding a peek into my future. Ding! A timid bell on the timer slightly startled me. I pulled my hair in a loose ponytail and then slowly looked at the test—my life changed that moment. Only three months after being married, I was pregnant. The honeymoon was barely over and Jalen and I were already going to have a baby. I looked down at my firm stomach and thought about everything that it meant to be pregnant. Would this body that he loved so much be gone forever? Would I be an awful mother? What was Jalen going to think?

I dialed the phone with my right hand and rubbed my belly with the left. "Hey Ann, this is Mel. Where is Jalen? Can you have him come to the phone please—it is kind of important?" Ann was my husband's receptionist. She was an absolutely delightful fifty-something year old lady with a nurturing motherly personality. I hired her immediately after meeting her and both Jalen and I had quickly developed a rather close knit relationship with her.

"Hey Princess—I was just thinking about you? What's up?" Jalen had a voice that could melt any woman over the phone. There was an awkward silence and he spoke out almost melodically "Mel??"

"What is the one thing that you could hear right now that would change your life the most, Jalen?" I asked him. I had to know if he would be happy about this or not. "Mel, don't tell me that Popeye's is going out of business" that had always been a joke between us. Jalen would die if he could not get his weekly fix of Popeye's.

"No baby, I'm serious."

"I don't know—maybe if we won the lottery…," he was still being silly.

"Well J, I think we won the lottery-" I replied. "The baby lottery."

There was a long piercing silence on the phone and then a shriek came across the line. An awkward thud came across the phone as it dropped and then in the background my husband began to laugh, and celebrate with his staff. I took a long deep breath of reassurance as I realized that he was very happy about this.

"It's going to be a boy, baby—no a girl, no a boy—you know it doesn't even matter." Jalen was ecstatic and I was too. "Come up here Mel, so I can give you a pregnancy test here in the office—can you come now, I am done for the day anyway."

"I am on my way baby! Try not to lose your mind waiting on me."

I slowed my car down to pull in my usual parking space next to Jalen's at his office. There was a cute little Infiniti parked in my space, however I paid no attention to it because that happened often. Preparing to park it elsewhere, I put my car in reverse, and started to back into another space just as the same familiar face from my wedding appeared. She picked up her pace to a girly jog in high heels immediately after seeing me; quickly she approached me, looking as trashy as ever.

Nausea built in my stomach as she began to speak to me saying, "Hey gurl!! I go from never seeing you to seeing you often—I wonder if that's a sign." I immediately thought to myself. "Yeah it's a sign that I should stay at home". The conversation between us was weird and I quickly decided to make it as short as possible. I continued to look around as I said, "I know uhmm—I never caught your name."

"Alexandra—everyone here calls me Alex"

"Okay Alex, see ya around", I replied hoping she would just walk away so I could park. She grinned slyly and kind of whispered, "You sure will".

She had no idea that I heard what she said but I read her lips as clear as day, she was definitely up to no good. While reversing and looking for a new spot, I realized that Alex walked up to the Infiniti that was in my parking space, looked right at me and climbed in. While, originally I did not care about someone parking in my space, rage came over me at that moment. Alex was intentionally working my nerves and I knew it. As she pulled off, I pulled into my designated space and sat as I thought for a second.

There was a quick hard tap on the windows followed by, "Girl, I'm in there waitin' on you and you sitting out here—you better get your butt in my office." I looked up at Jalen standing there, as handsome as ever, with a huge smile on his face. Every one of those pretty white teeth of his was seeing the light of day. I slowly climbed out of the car and decided not to reveal what had happened. Something inside told me that I would find out more by not even asking.

As I walked into the office, all of the employees were looking at me with wishful smiles on their faces. I looked at Jalen and said, "Baby, please tell me that you haven't told everyone yet. We don't even know if I am pregnant."

"Baby, I know you are. I knew it a while ago—I could feel it. I am only giving you the test for confirmation. Here take this cup and go into my bathroom in my office. Nurse Mae will come in there and test it." Jalen kissed my cheek and went to finish up his last patient. 'I will be back in a sec, Mel".

I fidgeted with my fingers as I waited on Mae to come in and test my urine. While waiting, I noticed Jalen's planner laying on his desk open to today's date. I thought about my encounter in the parking lot and curiosity drew me into taking a look at his calendar—just to be sure. As I peered at the day I realized that not only was there no mention of the tramp in the parking lot—but there was no mention of anything. It was empty, accept for a few asterisks written in on it. I assumed that it was some type of code that Jalen used that only he knew of.

"Okay where is the specimen?" Mae asked. "I can't wait to find out."

"Hey, Mrs. Mae! It's in the bathroom." I watched her walk hurriedly to Jalen's office restroom. "Mae, I met a patient outside—she was really nice. Do you know an Alex? Tall, cute shape, kind of provocative?"

"Honey yeah! She's been a patient here for a few months now. She always has something wrong with her. Every time I look up she's right—" Mae stopped speaking suddenly as if she realized that she had already said too much.

"Uhmm, I should be through with this test in a couple of seconds. Are you ready??"

"No let's wait for Jalen to get here. That way we can hear the results together. So what were you saying about Alex?"

I could tell that Mae was uncomfortable now. She tried to busy herself with picking up the test kit that she had brought into the office with her. "I wasn't saying much of anything sweetie. Girl, my legs have been hurting me something awful. I will go get Dr. Sparks so I can let the cat out of the bag." As Mae, walked off her wide nursing shoes squeaked and you could here the swish of her thighs rubbing together.

After what felt like about five minutes, Mae and Jalen walked into the room. Jalen sat on his desk anxiously looking as if he was about to check into a basketball game. "Okay, Mae lay it on us!! Am I going to be a baby's daddy?"

"Well, not now." Mae said with a look of disappointment on her face. Jalen's shoulders dropped in defeat. "But you will in about eight and a half months!!!"

My husband picked me up and swung me around in circles. I held him tightly and imagined how our lives were about to change. This was supposed to be a moment of celebration; however I was greatly distracted by my thoughts of Alex. "Well Jalen—you are really stuck with me now." I spoke to Jalen in a loving way, hiding my true insecurities about Alex.

He looked deep in my eyes as if he knew what I needed to hear and replied, "Baby I am stuck with you, stuck on you, and there's no place I'd rather be than with you." We kissed and sealed the moment that changed our lives forever.

As I lay on my bed, I looked at the black and white wedding photo of us on the wall and thought about how quickly my belly grew over the past few months. I watched helplessly as my favorite jeans slowly became a thing of the past. My hormones raged, causing me to experience severe ups and downs daily. Jalen tried to be very supportive of me throughout most of the pregnancy. He made food runs, ran my bath, rubbed my feet, and helped around the house when he was able to be home. However, his private practice had also increased its business and he found himself working more than ever. I started feeling very lonely at times, and growing resentful of the little person that I was sharing my body with.

Every time I found myself complaining about my situation, I thought about all that I had to be thankful for: a half a million dollar home, a wonderful husband that spoiled me with my every wish, and a thriving catering business that required no labor on my part. I had all of this going for me and still unhappiness lived in my gut and loneliness grew in my heart. My thoughts were interrupted by the phone ringing. I looked at the caller ID prepared to ignore the call, it was Kaiya.

"Hey! I almost didn't answer the phone Ky—what's up!"

"How's my baby boy? Is he kicking today? Let's go baby shopping." Ky had a habit of asking a list of questions and not waiting on the answer to either of them.

"I wish I would take my big butt out today—girl please!" I answered her sarcastically but inside I was so glad that she called. Kaiya was my rock. She and I had been friends almost forever. We met on the first day of school in kindergarten and had been tight every since. Though she could usually see through me to my emotions, I was determined not to let her know just how depressed I really was—so I hid it in my voice. "We can go out for food though. Do you have anymore clients today?"

After ending my conversation with Kaiya, I rolled out of bed and began to dress myself. I peered at my closet and then at the full length mirror that hung on the closet door. Pregnancy had done wonders for my hair; it was longer and shinier than it had ever been. My hips had spread somewhat, but I was still very shapely. My complexion was a clear mahogany and my eyes twinkled—though my spirit felt dull. I pouted my lips in the mirror and struck a sexy pose. As I did this, I heard a vibrating coming from Jalen's pants pocket. He must have forgotten his two-way.

I pulled it from the dress pants hung on his lazy boy. "Don't forget our lunch date—bring your appetite" was displayed on the screen. I wasn't sure whether this was an important message or not so I called Jalen at the office to remind him and to let him know where his two-way was just in case he missed it.

"Ann, could you put Jalen on the phone please." I waited while Ann got Jalen to the phone. As I waited, I grinned at the thought of how Ann would stop whatever Jalen was doing when I called. She was a sweet lady. Jalen came to the phone, and said hello in a voice that still gave me butterflies.

"Hey Princess, how's my son?"

"He's kicking up a storm. What are you doing for lunch?"

"Nothing, I am going to have to work through lunch. I hate I can't see you—but I will be swamped all day."

"I understand." The fact that he rejected seeing me before I asked was like a red flag to me. "You left your two-way here. Do you need it?"

"Just leave it in my pants pocket, okay Mel. Don't you be snooping," he seemed a little more distressed about it than he should have been. "Matter of fact—I am on my way home to get it."

I thought about everything that had just been said on the phone and realized that Jalen went from being too busy to see me, to having time to come and pick up his two-way just to keep me from looking at it.

"Princess...Mel are you there?"

"Yeah Jay, I hear you. See ya in a minute." I hung up the phone immediately without even waiting to hear good-bye from him. I didn't want to be home when he got there, so I put the pager back and began to dress quickly.

In the foyer of my home, I checked my appearance one more time before walking out of the door. My hair was pulled back into a trendy loose ponytail with 2k teardrop earrings that Jalen had bought months earlier framing my face. I was glowing in my pregnancy. Several minutes of deliberation led me to a Baby Phat jogging suit; I looked classy, sporty, and sexy. Though, I looked nice and was able to fix myself up nicely—emotionally, I was a mess. Slowly, I closed the door behind me and hopped into my red BMW with my eyes hid behind my shades.

Ky and I really enjoyed our lunch dates. She had always been the life of the party, so when we were together I could always relax and just be myself. Today, between small bites, I told Kaiya how I had been feeling, expecting her to tell me that it was my hormones and that everything would get better soon. It was then that Kaiya pointed out that she had only seen Jalen once in the past four months of my pregnancy. She further explained that this was a time when he should have been around the most. I quickly began to feel the need to defend my husband, though in my heart I knew that she was right.

"Girl you know Jalen, is a Family Physician. This winter time air has everybody sick. My baby has been busy trying to save the world." I spoke with humor in my voice in an effort to hide my true feelings.

"Mel, you need to wake up. You ain't nobody's fool. The office closes at five everyday, so starting at six every day he needs to be home with you. But I'm going to stay out of it. I'm your girl so if you like it—I love it!" The entire time that Kaiya spoke, I looked down and picked with my nails. Once she completed her sentence I looked back up at her and quickly changed the subject, "Let's go to the shop—I need my hair done."

As Ky and I rose from the table my knees trembled with realization that Jalen was never home, even after business hours. I was ready to go home, but I could tell that Ky was worried about me and I didn't want to give her any inclination that she was right or that I was concerned. Most of all, I didn't want her worrying about me, so I gathered my things with a smile and continued the day with her.

Kaiya was a wonderful hair dresser; she was probably the best in town. As I left her shop, I felt revived. My hair was full and bouncy, and for the first time in months, I felt like I looked nice. I went directly to Jalen's office after leaving Ky's. Once there, I carefully looked over the parking lot for the red Infiniti that had recently been showing up and ruining my days. Much to my delight, the car was no where to be found. I pulled into the space labeled "Mrs. Starks" and smiled at the sign.

As I walked into the office, I was greeted by many of the nurses leaving for late lunches. I stopped at Ann's desk to say hello and asked her to let Jalen know that I was waiting on him in his office. Right before I walked away, Ann looked at me in a motherly way and said, "Babies make it all worth it." I shook my head in an agreeable fashion and slowly turned to continue the walk to Jalen's office feeling perplexed.

I thought about Ann's comment and wondered whether my face showed the distress that I'd been feeling inside. I wondered if she had gone through this before. I wondered if she knew what I was going through or maybe what I was about to go through. Whatever the reason, I appreciated her concern and the hope that her comment offered me.

"Snap out of it, babe!" I was startled by Jalen's fingers snapping in my face. He leaned over and kissed me while running his fingers through my hair. "You are the finest pregnant woman I have ever seen Melany Starks."

"Thank you, Dr. Starks—you ain't half bad yourself." His scent was intoxicating. Truly, he was a magical man with a spell on me that was unbreakable. "Make sure you get home quickly this evening—we need a night out."

"I will be there ASAP, Mel." I watched Jalen's lips as they moved and kissed him as soon as he finished his sentence.

"I will make reservations Dr. Starks, and afterwards I may need a full check-up." I spoke slowly and seductively, determined to bring the spark back to my relationship. "I am looking forward to it honey." Jalen whispered. "Baby I have to get back to work now, that is if you want me to get home on time. I will see you at six." Jalen turned, and I watched him walk away strong and confident. His office was a mess. Files were strewn all over the place, leaving room for nothing on his desk except what was left of his lunch. The Tupperware was teal—and it did not look familiar. I assumed that Ann brought him lunch. The thought passed as quickly as it came, and I shuffled out of his office.

"Thanks for feeding my husband, Ann." I managed to get the words out. Just before walking out the door. I looked over my shoulder at Ann, and noticed a puzzled look on Ann's face as she replied. "Sweetie, I didn't bring any food today, but don't worry I will tomorrow."

This didn't sit right with me. I wasn't exactly comfortable with just anyone bringing my husband cooking from home. That was just a little too personal in my opinion. There shouldn't have been one broad there familiar enough to be doing all that. If he was hungry, he could have called the catering business we own to get food; or he could have called me to get food. I would have to talk to him about that later—or better yet—take better care of his lunch from here on.

The red numbers on the alarm clock in our room were burning my eyes. It read 7:08 and my husband was still not home. I sat on our bed dressed in his favorite dress. It too was red and it fit every curve on my body to perfection. Jalen always said that I was the only pregnant woman he knew that could wear a dress like this and still blow the room away. It was slinky, clingy, sexy, and very uncomfortable. I held my high heels in my lap. The heels on them were only about 2 inches high but with me being this far long in my pregnancy, they too were uncomfortable. I had swept my hair up and pinned it away from my face and even put on a little make-up and lip gloss for this occasion. When I realized that Jalen had definitely missed our reservations, a single tear ran down my face and rested on my dress.

"What could be more important than me?"

"Nothing Mel, I am so sorry for being late." Jalen replied in a remorseful tone.

I hadn't heard him come in and I certainly didn't realize that I was speaking my thoughts out loud. Jalen approached me with his arms extended. He helped me up off of the bed by my hands, grabbed me around my waist and kissed me softly. "Mel, I had a very sick patient to come in at 4:58 and I could not turn him away. I didn't finish seeing him until about 5:45, Victor has a new stalker so I had to give him a ride somewhere, and the traffic was heavy coming home. But I did do something special to try to make up for it. Grab your coat."

I reached and picked up the coat that I had ready to go. Not that one—this one. As I turned to see what coat Jalen was speaking of, he handed me a beautiful floor length mink coat. It was stunning. I gasped and put it on, smiling the entire time. Jalen had stopped to pick it up on the way home. That quickly, I forgot just how late he was and everything seemed okay.

"Okay babe—you look beautiful—let's go." Jalen spoke softly to me increasing the spell that he held over me. "We missed our reservations, Jalen. Where are we going to go now?" I inquired. Jalen gave me a smug grin then replied, "I called and took care of that. Our table will be ready whenever we arrive. You know how I do." My baby had all of the bases covered.

The cold air beat against my skin causing me to put my hands in the pockets of my new coat. Inside the left pocket, I felt a box. I took it out and told Jalen that there was something in the pockets of the coat, knowing all along that it was a gift for me. He looked at me, smiled and said, "I know baby, go ahead and open it."

I opened the box and awed at the beautiful tennis bracelet adorned with flawless princess cut diamond. I was speechless. "Mel, I know you have been having the baby blues and I just wanted to brighten your spirits. Think of this as a symbol of my love and appreciation for you."

"It didn't take all of this Jalen, I only need you. But since you went through all of this trouble, I'll take it!" I giggled like a school girl as I spoke to my husband. "Thanks baby!" Jalen's chest stuck out the rest of the ride to the restaurant while I rode alongside with a big toothy smile on my face.

Just after we pulled into *Madison's*, the restaurant where we had our very first date, I leaned over and kissed Jalen. He came around to my side, opened the door for me, and we walked into the restaurant hand-in hand. They seated us at the familiar romantic candlelit table and I took a quick survey of the room. In the far corner, glaring at us was a painfully familiar face. Alex was sitting at a table alone with one drink sitting in front of her. The drink was seemingly untouched, and there was no silverware at the table. Not many people come to expensive restaurants only to drink alone.

She never broke her stare, even when I looked directly at her. It was as if she wanted me to know that she was there. Her weave was long and a slightly different texture and color from that of her natural hair. She sat with her ankles crossed and her chin lightly supported with her left hand. Her lips were tight and her highly expensive attire somehow looked cheap on her. Even though I tried—I could not ignore her. No, she was not as cute as I; however she was definitely a force to be reckoned.

Jalen noticed me staring across the room and followed my stare to see what had stolen my attention. After Jalen spotted Alex, he laughed nervously and said "baby let's try to enjoy ourselves." He didn't wave at her, he didn't speak to her he just looked away from her—placing seemingly all of his attention on me. This was very odd to me. Alex was his patient, yet he didn't even attempt to speak to her. Jalen was always good at greeting his patients outside of the office. He would usually take a few moments just to make small talk with them. So I spoke up out of curiosity, "Jalen, aren't you going to speak to your patient?"

"No. That girl gets on my nerves Mel. She is a difficult patient and I really don't feel like talking to her right now." He took the bait. I was careful to word the question so that he would not realize that it was an investigative interrogation. Once he answered the first question wrong, many more began to fill my head. "I thought you said she only came to your office once."

"She did—but I still remember her face—not her name." I got him again. Why was he lying about this woman? Nurse Mae had already told me that she had been a patient for sometime, and was always there—so I knew that Jalen was hiding something. All of a sudden I wasn't hungry.

The remainder of the dinner was a miserable blur. Jalen talked constantly in what I thought was an attempt to cover up the ugly situation that was brewing. Alex sat and watched us attentively for about twenty minutes and then left the restaurant. Her drink remained, seemingly untouched. We stayed another hour or so in complete silence and finally left awkwardly. The ride home was very quiet, Jalen knew I was upset and became upset at me being upset. He looked at me, pursed his lips and said, "That's why women can't keep a good man. I go all out of my way to do something nice for you and the only thing you can think about is some broad that I can't even stand. You just let some woman that I don't even really know, ruin our evening. You got a good man, Mel. I don't deserve to be double questioned every time you get a little jealous about something. You don't think I knew that you were in there trying to check up on the things I told you and trying to catch me up in some lies. You are pretty pathetic. I know one thing—next time I won't even waste my time on you. I got better things to do. I can't wait to get out of this car with your trifling..." Jalen didn't finish his sentence. It was as if he knew that he was only making things worse for himself. I did not dignify his reaction with a response; to me the proof was in his defensive approach to things. If he wasn't guilty of anything, why was he so angry? I laid my head back on the headrest and closed my eyes; we rode in silence the rest of the way home.

As we walked through the door of our home, the temperature was warm but it didn't overcome the cold tension between my husband and me. Jalen immediately got on his cell phone and retreated to his study. Shortly thereafter I heard him yell that he was going with Victor to the sports bar as he slammed the door on his way out. Going to the sports bar usually meant that they were going to chase skirts. I went upstairs changed into my pajamas and went to bed with my back to Jalen's side of the bed. No words could express the sickness that I felt inside. I rubbed my belly for hours until finally, I drifted to sleep.

CHAPTER 3
▼

It felt like years had passed since I had gotten a good full night of sleep. Kylen had taken the majority of my time since his birth about ten weeks earlier. He was a beautiful little boy, with a full head of hair and eyes that sparkled like Jalen's. My new joy was the prince of the Starks family, showered with gifts and love from everyone Jalen knew. Now months after his birth, Kylen seemed to have fixed everything that was wrong in my life.

As I lay in the bed, thoughts began to race through my mind. I thought about the months that had led up to now. I had spent the last part of my pregnancy alone and waiting on Jalen to come home at night. Over my last trimester, the gifts increased as the loneliness grew. For every argument or night alone, I received a new "token of his appreciation". While the gifts were nice, I missed the joys of Couples Lamaze, baby shopping with Jalen, and decorating Kylen's new room with Jalen. At times, I even regretted being pregnant due to the loneliness that I felt; however everything changed the moment that Kylen entered this world.

Jalen spent more of his time home now. He helped with the baby, and acted as if things between us were really okay. Kylen came into this world and brought peace into our troubled home.

The smile provoking thoughts were interrupted by the ringing of the telephone. Jalen was busy with the baby, so I answered it. No one replied to my greeting when I answered the phone and the disconnecting click followed soon after. Only seconds after I hung up the phone Jalen rushed into the room, looked at his watch and said, "Honey, I think Kylen is hungry. I need to go to the office. I have a patient who just paged me. I think she's real sick. Do you need anything before I leave?" Jalen handed me the baby as he spoke hurriedly.

"No Jalen, thanks for checking with me. Be careful going to work. Kylen kiss your daddy bye-bye." Jalen leaned over and kissed our son on the cheek. I extended my cheek to receive the same favor from my husband but he quickly walked away, grabbed his coat, and headed out of the door.

No more than 45 seconds after his exit, the phone rang again. "Hello? Hello?" I answered with clear frustration in my voice this time. The calls were coming from a private number; the caller must have purposely blocked the number. Again, there was silence followed by the dial tone. My mind quickly shifted to Jalen as I placed the phone on the hook. He seemed to have left very suddenly, and it was very unconventional for him to go to the office on a Sunday. Worry clouded my mind and doubt quickly filled my eyes in the form of tears. I needed some kind of reassurance and something to take my mind off of the negative vibes that I was getting from these phone calls. I picked up the phone and dialed without thinking about who I was calling. My fingers chose seven numbers as my mind raced over the possibility that my husband was out with another woman. I put the phone to my ear—not sure of whom to expect to answer.

"Hey this is Kaiya. I can't get to the phone right now, leave a message and I may return your call." Kaiya's voice mail picked up immediately before the line rang at all. The message on it was very cheerful—she must have left it on a good day. Kaiya was probably out with Mark; she and he had very little time together during the week because of the hours that Kaiya worked. Sunday was their day to spend time.

"Hey Ky! It's me. Call me whenever you can. I was just checking on you. Love ya," I spoke as cheerful as I could into Kaiya's voicemail.

I quickly began to dial another number, feeling a desperate need to communicate with someone.

"Hey Mama!" I said before she even said hello. My mother-in-law always took a long time to say hello. She would first have to check for the pause that you hear when telemarketers call. If she heard the silent pause, she would immediately hang up.

"Hey Melany! You okay? How's my grandson?"

I spent about five minutes speaking to Mama about Kylen and how much he had changed since she saw him last. She was just tickled to death to hear about her only grandchild, or her Puddin' as she called him. Jalen was an only child so Kylen had become her main topic of conversation. After talking about Kylen for a while, I tried to find a way to venture into a conversation about Jalen and me. He was the apple of her eye so it would definitely take finesse; nobody could make her believe anything bad about her Jalen.

"Mama, what was the hardest thing about marriage for you and Mr. Starks?"

"Baby, it was making it through the tough times that made marriage difficult. They are going to come and you have to be ready for them. Stay prayed up Mel, and be ready to stand by your husband through anything. He's gonna make mistakes; but as a wife with a child, you have to stay and try to work through them."

Mama's advice surprised me because she seemed so independent and here she was suggesting that I stay through anything. Though the advice that she was giving seemed a little absurd and biased, I pressed on with the subject, "What if your heart tells you that something isn't right?"

"Baby the heart doesn't matter much when you make a vow to God. The heart can lie to you—and people, Lord people, they will lie to you. Just hold on to your marriage Mel. It's what God wants from us. It ain't easy being somebody's wife, but Jalen is a good man and you are the perfect woman for him."

Mama paused, and then changed the subject to the dinner that she prepared that day. However, I didn't hear anything else that she said.

My mind was stuck wondering what was to come for my marriage. I thought about how hard things had been up to this point and became terrified at the thought of them getting any worse.

In the weeks that followed my conversation with Mama, Jalen and I spent plenty of time trying to rekindle the flame between us. While, I enjoyed the time, I couldn't help but feel as if we wouldn't ever be able to truly rekindle the fire, no matter how many sparks we made. We did not grow any closer during this time; we merely spent time together ignoring the obvious distance between us and talking about our family. As Kaiya always put it—we were ignoring the elephant in the room.

Months after Kylen's birth we began to have Lover's Lane. This had become a Saturday morning ritual for us that we initiated for the sole purpose of bringing the excitement back to our marriage. We would leave Kylen with his sitter, Reece, and go out for brunch and any other activities that involved spending time together as a not-so-newlywed couple. While I always looked forward to being with Jalen for these outings, I dreaded the moments of silence that we often experienced. Jalen went along with the idea and always planned something nice for us to do, however he seemed distant and detached while we were together, causing awkward moments of silence.

I started planning the day's topics of discussions in my head as I put the finishing touches on my hair and lip-gloss. I rechecked the pins that were holding my up-swept hair in place then adjusted my fitted dress to allow the seam to go straight down the middle of my back and the high split to go straight up the middle of my left thigh. I slid on my heels, struck a pose, and loved it. Full of confidence, I opened my bathroom door to reveal the results of all my hard work to Jalen. "Jalen baby, I must say—I look like a million…" Jalen was adjusting his tie in the mirror when I walked into the room, and his duffel bag was at his feet. He looked at me in the mirror and spoke.

"What baby? I didn't hear you."

"Jalen? Where are you going? Today is Saturday; we always go out together on Saturdays."

"Mel, I told you last week that I had a convention to go to this morning. It is a one-day convention so I should be home late tonight. My plane leaves in two hours and Victor is on his way to pick me up and take me to the airport." As he spoke, I racked my brain trying to remember any instance in which he may have mentioned a convention. I would have remembered it for sure—especially with it being on OUR day. He didn't mention it to me. I was sure of that.

"Jalen, you did not tell me about a damn convention. If you had I would not be standing here all dressed up looking like somebody's prom date."

"Mel, you don't listen. If you would just shut up and listen some times you would know everything that goes on with me. That's your problem—you're too worried about what I'm doing. I know I told you; it's your fault if you missed it."

Jalen grabbed his bag and walked past me, brushing my shoulder as he passed. I could actually feel the disgust coming off of him as he walked out the door. No kiss, no good-bye—just disgust. The slamming of the door shouldn't have startled me but it did. I stood still and looked around the room. I was frozen in one spot, waiting on the door to open and for Jalen to come back and kiss me good-bye. As I waited, the seconds turned to minutes. Finally, after a long ten minutes, my feet trudged to my bed. Slowly I removed every article of clothing that I'd put on just to look good for Jalen. I threw the shoes across the room. I let the dress drop to my ankles. The hairpins went somewhere behind the dresser and the lip-gloss went to the back of my hand. When there was nothing else to remove, I climbed into my bed full of weariness and waited on Reece to bring Kylen home.

I was awakened to the phone ringing; I smiled as I answered it expecting to hear Reece's voice. "Hi Jalen Starks please." The voice was pleasant and professional.

"Jalen isn't home. This is his wife. Is there a message?"

"Hi Mrs. Starks, this is the Hilton Towers Hotel and we are calling to confirm today's reservations. Will your husband still need his suite?"

I paused at the question and wondered what he would need with a suite for a one-day convention, if there really was a convention. He probably got it just in case he needed it. I then replied to the young lady on the line, "Yes, please keep the room reserved and available for Jalen. Oh, and thanks for calling."

"No problem and thank you." I placed the phone on the hook and stared at it. I wanted to pick it up and call Jalen. I wanted to gain the reassurance that the room was reserved "just in case". However, fear held me hostage. Calling Jalen and questioning him would definitely upset him. He would assume that I didn't trust him, and accuse me of snooping. He would tell me that he told me about the room and again make me feel as if I don't ever listen. My heart was telling me that something was wrong; I simply could not face it—at least, not yet.

I spent the rest of the day spoiling Kylen. We went to the park, to visit Kaiya, and shopping. I showered him with all of the energy that I couldn't give to my husband. Kylen had his father's eyes; he represented a piece of Jalen that actually loved me back. Every time my cellphone rang I answered it hoping to hear Jalen's voice; he didn't call. The sun was setting as Kylen and I pulled into our long circular driveway. I made my way to the front door while I looked at our house and wanted so badly for it to become a warm loving home.

After singing Kylen to sleep, I placed him in his crib and looked long and deep into his face. He was worth every thing that Jalen and I were going through. With Kylen asleep, I looked up the long hallway to the bedroom that I shared with Jalen; I dreaded going in. I dreaded the cold sheets and the silence of the room. I slowly moved towards it leaving a trail of tears that led from Kylen's room into my dreams.

Blinking quickly as my eyes adjusted to the brightness in the room, I aroused from my sleep to see Jalen preparing for bed. It was three a.m. and Jalen was getting dressed as silently as possible. He slid into the bed with me as if nothing had happened and we lay back to back. That night I slept with a stranger.

Chapter 4

I pulled the BMW up into the parking lot that led to my husband's practice. I drove slowly to the space that was designated to me. The sign was now missing and a Tahoe was occupying the spot. "Victor knows better than to park in my spot—I don't care if the sign is missing," I fussed out loud to myself. Victor's law office was located in Jalen's building. He had complained for months about not having his own parking space in a building that he paid to use. I knew it wouldn't be long before he actually got one.

He was a single, brilliant attorney and considered a big catch throughout the city. Victor went through women like I went through shoes. Because he was single, he spent a lot of time at our house eating dinner and hanging out with Jalen. He often brought his dates over to get our approval of them, though we never saw one more than a couple of times. Victor and Jalen were like brothers and I loved him as a brother as well. Sighing, I pulled into the parking space located next to the Tahoe.

I checked my appearance in the mirror before getting out of the car. I never came to see Jalen looking a mess. He was always very particular about appearances. Over my right shoulder, I saw a Red Infiniti reflected in my rearview mirror. The car was parked directly behind mine, and close enough for me to look the driver in the eyes. The eyes that met mine were full of anger and hatred. The silent confrontation intimidated me for about ten seconds—then suddenly the entire face of the driver came into focus. It was Alex. Though she had changed her appearance greatly, the affect was still the same. She was nice looking, however something about her attire or hair was always just a little forced and off. On this occasion, she wore a strawberry blonde weave though her roots were auburn and her hair had been swept up loosely; similar to how I would wear my hair often. She had thickly lined her lips with black eyeliner, commanding the attention away from the other softer features of her face.

I looked down at the shoes I had on and realized that they were not exactly "throwing" shoes. I removed one of them and glanced over my shoulder again as I began to remove the second one. She was gone; she had vanished into thin air just as quickly as she appeared. I looked carefully around the parking lot for some sign of where she had gone but there was no sign of her whatsoever. I smiled at myself and joked out loud, "I knew she didn't want none of this." Laughing, I thought about the fact that I had never had a fight in my life and was terrified at the thought of actually having to fight anyone. I had a lot at stake this time though. Alex was a threat to my marriage and therefore a threat to me. If a fight was what she wanted—a fight is what she would get.

Looking around again, I slowly opened my car door and put both feet outside of the car to put on my shoe. Once it was secure, I adjusted my hair, grabbed my Kelly bag and strutted into the office. My strut was long and confident just in case Alex was watching. As I made my way to Jalen's office, I stopped to see Ann. I greeted her before she saw me, "Hey Ann! How you been?"

"Well, hello Melany. I didn't hear you come in."

"I didn't mean to startle you. Can I see the appointments and patients for today? I have to send confirmations and thank you notes." This wasn't out of the ordinary because I performed administrative tasks for Jalen regularly. But this time I had to know if Alex had been in to see Jalen. I looked over the appointment list and realized that Alex had not been in as a patient. "Ann, I saw Alex in the parking lot. Was she in today? Because she is missing from this sheet?"

"No, I haven't seen Alex today and I have been here all day. Maybe she had business somewhere else in this building, but definitely not in here."

"Okay thanks Ann," I walked away perplexed. Had she followed me just to intimidate me? What kind of a woman was I dealing with?

I walked into Jalen's office and was greeted by Victor, "Hey sis!"

I playfully punched him and fussed, "Don't hey me punk! You got some nerve, parking your big old truck in my spot. Where is my husband?"

"He's writing a prescription. He should be right back. We were about to go to eat, are you coming?" Jalen walked in right as Victor finished the sentence. He quickly interceded, "Man you know Mel can't roll with us. She has to pick up Kylen in a little bit." He kissed me on the cheek and sat on his desk directly in front of me; allowing his legs to swing as he smiled big.

"Well, since Jalen already answered for me, the answer is no Victor, I will not be joining you. Thanks for asking though." I gave Jalen a stern look for his rudeness and then asked, "Jalen, can I speak to you for a minute?"

"Sure babe. Hey Vic, I will be out in a second just wait on me in the car." As the door closed behind Victor, I took a deep breath and asked, "Jalen, did you know that somebody stole my sign?"

"Mel, your sign wasn't stolen. I took it down. Before you go shootin' off at the mouth listen to me. This is a place of business. I only put your name on the sign because I assumed that you would be here working. There are people who lease space here and they don't have spaces. It was okay when you were here working and visible. Well, now that you are here a lot less and doing most of the work from home—you don't need a sign. You know you only want one to show off anyway. Also, while we are talking about this—stop all of that popping up and being nosy. If you are coming here to see me; call first. This is a place of business and you need to act like it."

His speech caught me completely off guard. I looked at him with one eyebrow raised and checked him, "Whoa Jalen. There is just a little too much steam coming off of you right now. First of all, I could care less about the little sign. Second of all, I don't need to show off at your business when I have my own business that I can show off, don't get it twisted. Third of all, popping up is what I do—if you don't like it—tough. So tell your girl Alex to be careful coming all up in through here. I don't know who you think you talking to. I'll come up here when I want to come up here. Now what?" I walked off as I completed my sentence. I was proud of how I stood up for myself but my heart ached from the episode. I didn't look back at Jalen to see his expression. It didn't matter anymore. I heard the elevator doors close behind me and made my way to my hair appointment.

"Girl, no he didn't. Jalen knows he was dead wrong for that." Kaiya was just as surprised at Jalen's antics as I was. As she shampooed my hair, she maintained eye contact with me and followed the story. "No Ky," I replied, "that ain't even the best part."

"It better be—you already done told me too much. What else happened?"

"So…I'm checkin' my hair in my rear view right?" I began to tell Kaiya about the confrontation I had today. "And I see the Red Infinti pull up behind me ultra-close. Girl, it was Alex. This broad was looking at me like she wanted to do something to me. You know I am the last person to fight, but Ky I had to go on and take off my shoes."

"Melany Lanae," Ky always called me by my first and middle name when she was excited. "Don't tell me that you got into a fight. You know you are too old to be fighting anybody."

"Naw girl. When I looked up from kicking my shoes off—she was gone. I don't know whether I bluffed her out, or she was playing games to start with. But I told Jalen that I will pop up when I feel like it and to tell Alex to watch her back." By this time, Kaiya had completely stopped what she was doing and was looking me in my face in disbelief. She thought for a second and then replied in a concerned tone, "Mel, how far does this have to go for you to wake up."

"Wake up from what? Alex is not a threat. She is just annoying." I started to feel the need to change the subject. "Anyway, I am married to Jalen and we have a child, it's more complicated than a regular boyfriend/girlfriend relationship. I gotta try to make it work for Kylen, if for no other reason." My vocal tone must have convinced Kaiya to let the subject go. She went back to shampooing my hair, saying no more about my marital situation.

As I was preparing to leave the salon, my cell phone rang. I looked at the phone and saw that it was Jalen. I had no desire to speak to him at that moment so I ignored the call, and went to pick up Kylen. About one hour later, Jalen called again. I answered the phone as dryly as I could, "Yeah."

"Mel baby—where are you?"

"Mindin' my business and staying out of yours Jalen," that was about the best thing that I could come up with at the moment. He laughed at my played out comment and replied, "I guess I had that one coming. Baby, I need to talk to you. It's very important. Please come straight home after you get Kylen. Please." I wanted so badly to continue to be mean, but something in Jalen's voice sounded seriously urgent. I agreed to get home as quickly as possible and hung up the phone.

Immediately after walking into the house, I had an eerie feeling that something was definitely wrong. Jalen met me in the den and took Kylen into his arms. His eyes were red and swollen from crying and his face looked flushed. He hugged Kylen for what seemed like two minutes before he put him down and began to speak to me. "Mel, I know that your mother died a while ago and my Mama has been very special to you for some time now. So please try to look at this from a positive standpoint, if possible."

"Quit beating around the bush, Jalen. Is Mama okay? Where is she?" The tears were already forming in my eyes.

"Mel, my Mama has cancer. She has been fighting it for sometime now, but she found out today that it has spread to too many of her vital organs. There is nothing left for them to do except to try make her comfortable until she passes." Jalen's news floored me literally. My knees became weak, and I found myself sitting on the floor with no recollection of how I got there. I broke out in a cold sweat and the tears flowed uncontrollably. Mama meant the world to me. She came into my life and partnered with my Mom, who had passed previously and was still a very big part of my life. She never treated me as an in-law. I needed her in my life and I could not imagine adjusting to losing another mother.

Jalen gently lifted me up off of the floor and placed me on the sofa. "Mel, she is going to need you to be stronger than this. She has asked that no one be sad while she's around and that we put all of our energy into enjoying life with her in it. She asked me to bring Kylen to spend a few weeks with her as soon as possible, while she is still feeling normal."

"Okay J. We can take him tomorrow if you like."

"Mel, you are not ready to face her yet. I am going to take Kylen tomorrow. You stay here and rest. I have ordered a spa day for you tomorrow, it'll help relax you. By the way baby, I am so sorry about today. I have been really stressed lately. I shouldn't have snapped at you like that."

At this moment, Jalen's apologies meant absolutely nothing to me. The argument that we had that day meant even less to me. All that mattered was that I was losing my mother again and there was nothing that I could do about it. Immediately, I picked up the phone and called her. As the phone rang I cleared my throat and prepared myself to speak in a fashion that respected her wish to not have to deal with sad people. I heard her pick up the phone and the normal "telemarketer check" pause was ended with a hello from Mama. "Hey Mama. I talked to Jalen today and I was calling to see if you needed anything from us right now?"

"Mel?" She always said my name to make sure that she caught my voice. "All I need is to see my grandson for a while. When is he coming?"

"Jalen is bringing him tomorrow Ma. I will send him enough clothes to last a couple of weeks or so. If you need anything else—give me a call."

"Okay baby. And Mel…" she paused, "I love you!"

"I love you too Mama." I replied softly and hung up the phone as tears ran down my face.

The next few days without Kylen were very lonely. I missed him dearly and called to speak to him daily. He was just over a year old, and unable to talk so I would call and just listen to him yell gibberish into the phone. Every day Mama seemed to have a little playmate over for Kylen. This really made me happy. The fact that that Mama was taking care of two babies let me know that she was still feeling pretty well.

Today as I spoke to Kylen, I began to feel very ill. It came on suddenly and hit me hard. I immediately finished the phone call with Kylen and went into the bathroom just in case it wasn't just nausea. As I sat on the edge of the sink, I realized that I was not just a little late for my cycle; I was way late for it. In all of the stress that I had been experiencing—I hadn't thought too much about my missing period.

Panic rushed over my body and I began to search desperately for my calendar. As I counted the weeks my hands began to shake and I realized that I was quite possibly six weeks pregnant. The last time that I thought I was pregnant was with Kylen—I bought several pregnancy tests and two of them were still left under the sink. I grabbed it and immediately decided to take it. I waited for the results and said a short prayer asking God to help me to accept whatever it may read. I asked him to especially help Jalen accept the outcome. I ended the prayer and opened my eyes to a blue positive sign showing on the screen in bold color.

There were several thoughts that rushed to mind when I saw this result. The first thought was Jalen. He and I were very detached and barely able to hold it together for Kylen—how would this affect our marriage? Next, I thought about Mama, and whether she would be able to stick around long enough to hold this baby. Then I began to think about myself. The baby blues were pretty bad when Jalen and I were having problems during my first pregnancy. How would I cope with a pregnancy now that he and I were completely on the outs. At any rate, the results were in and I decided to pick up the phone to inform my husband.

"Hi Ann. Is Jalen around?"

"Sure Mel, hold a sec", the hold music began to play *I Heard it Through the Grapevine.*

"Hey Babe," Jalen answered the phone cheerfully.

"Hey J. I need to make an appointment for ASAP," I beat around the bush unable to find the words to tell Jalen the news. He paused curiously and then asked why I needed an appointment. "Well, I may be pregnant." Absolute silence followed my statement. There was no response from Jalen for about 20 seconds and then he finally replied, "That figures, Mel. You would pull something like this, trying to trap me. You can come on up here now."

"What does that mean? I would pull something like what? If I am not mistaken it took two and you were there with me when it happened."

"Yeah Mel, whatever. Are you coming or not?"

"Yeah," I answered him quickly and hung up the phone.

The ride to the office was long and nerve wrecking. I really didn't need a test to tell me that I was pregnant. I knew I was and Jalen's response completely surprised me. He didn't even wait to confirm the pregnancy before he went off on me. A few alternative options floated through my mind.

I could bypass the office and tell Jalen that I am not pregnant and then secretly schedule abortion; but I would not be able to live with that option. The guilt alone would kill me, plus I truly didn't believe in abortion, especially in my case. Option two, I could face what seemed to be the inevitable and separate from Jalen and deal with this pregnancy without the added stress of dealing with his bad attitude. That option was definitely not going to happen. I loved Jalen and my family too much to give up this quickly. Option three was to suck it up, deal with it and wait on Jalen to come around. This option was the obvious choice. I sighed at the thought of what I was about to endure, but smiled at the thought of having another blessing added to my life.

Walking into the building, I couldn't help but to look around expecting to see Alex's car in the lot. It not in sight; I then then decided to let my guard down. I walked straight into Jalen's office without stopping to talk to Ann today. I was just unable to muster up the strength to fake my happiness for others. Jalen walked into his office right behind me and closed the door behind him. He handed me the cup and sat on his desk as if he wanted to fill it right there in front of him.

"If you don't mind, I'll be right back." I spoke with out even looking at him and turned to go into his restroom. I filled the cup and stuck it out the door so I would not have to wait in the room with Jalen as he tested it. I decided to take my time coming out of the bathroom; at this moment I was truly intimidated by Jalen. I reapplied my lip gloss, smoothed my hair down, and freshened up. After a few minutes, I came out of the bathroom. Jalen was standing outside of the door with a sour look on his face. He looked at his feet and said, "It's positive."

"Okay, I'll see you later." I had to get away from him as quickly as possible. Before the levy that held the flood gates gave way. I was heartbroken and the tears were imminent. "Bye, Jalen."

"No you won't see me later. I need some time to think Mel. All of this is just too much. I am going to stay at Victor's for a few nights—just to clear my head."

"Yeah right", I replied as I turned on my heels and headed towards the door. "Tell Alex, I said hello." Tears streamed down my face as I stormed out of his office. On my way out, I picked up the monthly list of charges that I needed to submit and walked out the door without saying a word to anyone.

    The house was unbearably quiet that evening with Kylen away at Mama's and Jalen being somewhere "cooling off." Kaiya came over to keep me company and to help me with the work that I needed to do. She was cheerful and talkative this evening; though I tried, I was unable to return the favor. She noticed that I was a little quiet and began to speak to break the silence, "Why do you wait until the last minute to do this stuff anyway?"
    "Ky, I can't stand going up to that office with Jalen, so I put it off for as long as I can. Plus, with the way that man has been acting, he should be glad that I do it at all." The stack of checkout sheets to be billed was huge, there was no way that this would be completed tonight. As I flipped through the checkout sheets, Alex came to my mind. I began to look for one of her checkout sheets in the stack. According to the nurses' appointment log, she had been in a couple of times this month so there should have been a few checkout sheets there for her. After looking for some time, I realized that she did not have one sheet in the stack. I pulled her file up on the laptop and realized that she had not been billed for one single visit over the past few years. "Ky, Jalen and this Alex girl are really about to piss me off. Do you realize she ain't got one charge on her account? First, Jalen says he don't know her, then he does know her as a patient but can't stand her, now I see that she is a patient that get seen for free. There ain't even an insurance company being billed. He is seeing her for absolutely free; I mean ain't nobody paying for services rendered to this tramp. He is sleeping with her Kaiya. I know it. He had the nerve to tell me that he was going to stay at Victor's. He must think I'm some kind of a fool."
    "Girl, I wouldn't pay no attention to her. If Jalen is seeing her it will come out. He can only cover it up for so long. Even the perfect front plays out eventually. Where is he anyway?" Kaiya looked around

when she asked that as if she expected him to come out of the shadows. "He's never here anymore. I mean things seemed to get better after Kylen was born, but now they done got worse."

"I just told you he was at Victor's. He said that he needs some time to think."

"What does he have to think about? Alex. Girl, your husband makes me so dang sick sometimes. Oooh, I just want to ring his neck."

"Jalen said that he needs time to think because…" I paused, unable to bring myself to say the words again. "Ky, you are going to be an aunt—again."

"What? Oh my God. That is so good. I am so jealous." Kaiya took the information entirely different than I expected her to. She was happy for me and her happiness made me excited too. That was exactly what I needed from her, unwavering support. "Mel you know, I can't have kids so I look at all babies as a blessing. I don't care what Jalen tells you, these babies are brought into our lives for a reason. If Jalen wants to take his tail over to Vic's to pout about a blessing then let him. As far as you and me—we are going to celebrate."

"Thanks Ky." I watched Kaiya get up and walk over to the CD player and put in a CD. We danced for what seemed like hours. Realizing that we had to drive two hours in the morning to pick up Kylen, we both called it a night just after midnight. Kaiya stayed the night just to keep me company and we slept on the floor in the living room like we did when we were girls. She was the friend that I needed at a time when I needed her most. As I fell asleep, I thanked God for Kaiya and for the new blessing that was growing inside of me.

Chapter 5

My second pregnancy so far had been less eventful than the last one. Though Jalen and I were still on the rocks, in the rocks, and under the rocks—I had a certain peace this time that I did not have when I was pregnant with Kylen. Jalen stayed at Victor's for a week or so at the beginning of the pregnancy but came to grips with the fact that there would be another child coming whether he liked it or not and shortly thereafter, he came home. While he did try to be a supportive husband, the bridge between us was too severely damaged from all the mess that he already had put me through.

I found myself talking to Victor on several occasions, searching for a way to heal my marriage. I wanted to know what Jalen needed from me, and how I could please him as his wife. Victor always seemed to have the same reply after every conversation. He would look at me as if he felt sorry for me and would say," Mel, people only do what you let them do." After hearing that comment over and over again, it finally sunk in today and I hung up with Victor feeling like a brand new woman. I was glowing, with child, and determined to make the best of my situation.

I was lying in bed rubbing my belly when Kylen walked into the room and smiled at me. He had already learned how to say Mommy and he marched around the house all day singing it. I looked at him and rolled out of the bed, "Kylen, let's go get you dressed. You have to go to the doctor. Up we go!!!" I swung him around by his arms as I sang, "up we go." It was time for Kylen's eighteen-month appointment, and we needed to get out of the house in record time to keep from being late.

I quickly got dressed after dressing and feeding Kylen in an effort to leave the house before Jalen called and asked to accompany us. "Come on baby—let's go." I grabbed Kylen's hand and hurried towards the front door. As I grabbed the doorknob to leave, the phone began to ring. I knew it was Jalen wanting to go to the doctor with Kylen and me. He was an awful husband to me, but a wonderful and involved father to Kylen. Picking Kylen up and ignoring the ringing phone, I shuffled out the house.

My cell phone rang the whole time that we were riding to the pediatrician. Finally, I answered it as we pulled into the parking lot of Kylen's doctor's office, knowing it would probably be too late for Jalen to try to join us at that point. "Hello?" I answered making certain that Jalen heard the irritation in my voice. Jalen paused for a second before speaking, "Mel."

"Yeah, Jalen"

"I was wondering if you could reschedule Kylen's appointment and come spend some time with me." Jalen was speaking very softly as if he were trying to verbally seduce me. "I think we need some alone time."

"Jalen, it will have to wait. Kylen needs his shots and he needs this checkup today. Besides, I am already here at the office. I gotta go." I hung up the phone before Jalen could object. He was really tripping. Things weren't all that good between us. I still loved him and I enjoyed our alone time, when we had it. However, right then, I needed to be away from him.

I signed Kylen in at the check-in desk of the pediatrician and wondered why Jalen was so urgent about seeing me now and why he wanted me to reschedule an appointment for no reason. Did he miss me that much? What kind of a game was he playing? I handed the assistant my check for the co-pay and suddenly felt a hand on my shoulder, I spun quickly expecting to see Jalen but was unpleasantly stunned to see Alex. I angrily pulled my shoulder away from her grasp and glared at her. She had a little boy in her arms that appeared to be about the same age as Kylen. She grinned with a very white toothy smile and said, "So we meet again. Hey Mel, and hello there little Mr. Kylen. You look just like your daddy." She used a baby voice as she spoke to Kylen and reached out to grab his little hand. I quickly pulled Kylen away and moved him to the other side of me. I spoke to Alex, careful to maintain a hateful glare that obviously burned right through her. "Alex, I don't know why you make it a point to be every where that I am but this is gettin' real old—real fast. And that little number you pulled in the parking lot at the office almost got you hurt. Please believe me. We are not friends, we have nothing in common and most of all—I don't like you. Next time you want to make it a point to see me—don't."

"First of all Mel, you need to slow down. If I see you out, it's because I just so happened to run into you. You ain't all that for me to be running around chasing you. That day in the parking lot, I was there for a reason and believe me we have more in common than you know. So from here on when you see me—know this—I don't like you anymore than you like me. I only tolerate you…and I won't be doing that for too much longer."

"Well," I replied. "Tolerate me from over there somewhere." Without even looking at her, I shooed her away. Several people heard the commotion and began to stare. After gathering my composure, I picked my receipt up off of the desk and had a seat in the waiting room.

As I sat, with Kylen in my lap, I played a word game with him. I pointed to the clothes that he was wearing and called out the name of them so he could try to repeat it after me. Kylen quickly became uninterested in this game and climbed down from off of my lap. He pointed across the room and said, "Tase". I looked in the direction that he was pointing and realized that Alex was sitting in the part of the waiting room that claimed Kylen's attention. He seemed very familiar with Alex's little boy. "Mama, tase" Kylen repeated it again and pointed directly at Alex's child. Alex's mouth turned up into a sly grin and she seemed somewhat amused by what my child was saying. "Case what, Kylen?" I was unable to fully concentrate on what Kylen was trying to tell me because I was too busy glaring at Alex. As I tried to figure out what Alex was grinning about, a nurse opened the door and called out, "Alexandra and Chase Sanders". My heart began to beat quickly as I realized that Kylen seemed to know Alex's son. I looked at Kylen in an attempt to connect with him mentally, "What did you say baby?"

"Mama Tase," Kylen said it again and pointed out the window. I breathed a huge sigh of relief when I realized that he was merely speaking gibberish again. He continued to gab as I sat and thought about this whole Alex situation. How did she know Kylen? Was my husband the thing that she and I had in common? Was she really a threat to my marriage? How long had this been going on?

"Melany and Kylen Starks," my thoughts were interrupted by the nurse calling us to the back. I gathered our things and began to head back to the examination room, already exhausted from the day. As we walked, the nurse began to make small talk with me, first asking how my day had been. I tried to sound cheerful as I responded, "Good and yours?"

"It's been busy here at the office. Aren't you Dr. Starks' wife?"

"Yes, I am." I responded noticing how she quickly changed the subject. "Why? Do you know him?"

"Let's just say that I know of him. I hear he is a great Physician." The chubby nurse didn't make eye contact with me as she spoke. She seemed to know something that I didn't know. She led us into a spacious examination room and said, "Remove all of Kylen's clothes and someone will be in to weigh him shortly." She closed the door softly behind her and left the room. I could hear the squeak of her shoes with each step she took. I didn't move until I could no longer hear the squeak.

Minutes later, as I undressed Kylen, we sang the dress up song that he and I had made up together. It helped to temporarily get my mind off of the horrible day that it had been so far. When the song ended, I began to hear giggling in the hallway. The voices were quiet yet audible. I could easily make out what they were saying. "…And you mean to tell me that they are in rooms right next door to each other?", one voice questioned while laughing. The other voice answered, "Girl yes, right next door, they are sharing a man, a bill, and a doctor—honey his wife is better than me—I would have killed me a…." The door swung open and the nurse walked back into the room. She began to weigh Kylen and as I watched, my eyes burned with embarrassment. Everyone knew of my situation and people were talking. I looked like a fool around here and I was the laughing stock of the office.

I watched the nurse weigh my son wondering if she too knew of the fool that I was being for my husband. I wondered if she too would laugh at me as soon as she left the exam room. The more I wondered the heavier the burden got. As the reality of my situation began to weigh on me, the tears flowed from my eyes. At the end of Kylen's appointment, I walked away from that office for good, It would be the last time that I would show my face there. As I walked to the car, I remembered Victor's words. I would not let them continue to be entertained at my expense.

Kylen's appointment had tired him out so he slept the whole way home. I rode in complete silence thinking about my marriage and how it had managed to get to this point. I thought about the first time that I saw Jalen. My catering company was handling a party that he was having for his office. I met with him prior to the party to discuss their menu request and was stunned at how attractive he was. Jalen was smooth, organized, classy, polite, and successful. How did he become the abrasive, scattered, rude, and sneaky man that I now lived with?

When I pulled into the circular driveway of our home, I saw that Jalen was already there. This was unusual because he was never home this early in the day. I gathered up my things in one hand and Kylen in the other and made my way into the house and up to Kylen's bedroom. As I laid Kylen down for his nap—Jalen came and stood in the hallway behind me. "Hey Mel," Jalen began to speak as I walked past him out of the room. "Long day?"

"Longer than you could ever know Jalen."

"Well I have been waiting on you to get here. I have really missed hanging out with you. Do you have a moment?" Jalen was rubbing my cheek as he spoke. I quickly pulled away from his touch and replied, "Nope—not really. But maybe Alex does."

"Melany what does Alex have to do with this. Please don't start that. I don't want to argue; I only want to hold you tonight." As Jalen reached out to touch me, I felt a sickness in the pit of my stomach. The disgust built with every word that he spoke. "Melany, I know things have been a little rough between us and that I haven't been the most supportive husband throughout this pregnancy, but I am here now. I promise that from this moment on I will be everything that you need. Victor told me about the conversation that you all had and I don't want to lose you. Mel, you are my wife—my life and my heart." As Jalen finished his sentence, I felt my heart began to soften. I began to lose sight of that rage that I felt as I left the doctor's office today. The disgust in my stomach melted into doubt; doubt of my right to be angry. I felt great insecurity in my reason for not trusting my husband. Just as I moved to return the kiss that my husband had extended his lips to give, my feet froze in place. I thought about Victor's advice as it rang clearly in my head, "Mel, people only do what you let them do." I thought about the many times that I accepted Jalen's apologies twenty seconds after they were given without any proof of his sincerity. I thought about Alex and the audacity that she approached me with. Normally, that type of nerve is not present without reason.

Jalen's kiss met a cold cheek, as I turned my head in disgust. I replied, "No you didn't ask me what this has to do with Alex. You tell me. What does she have to do with us? Every time I look up, this broad is in my face or all up in my space…so you tell me what she has to do with us. Then, on top of all that, nurses at Kylen's doctor clowning me in my face over the fact that me and ya girl are sharing you and sharing a pediatrician. She was in the exam room right next to me. I felt like the biggest fool in there sitting with my child in the waiting room with your skank." As I spoke, Jalen wore an expression of shame mixed with shock. He opened his mouth as if to reply but I wasn't through with him yet. As my confidence built I lowered my tone, smiled smugly and continued, "I tell you what—how about this? You explain what the hell is going on or explain to Kylen why yo ass ain't around no more. The next words that I need to hear from you need to be "Here's what's going on". If you ain't got that for me—then you need to pack up all yo junk and roll up outta here. I don't care where you go—just get the hell out of my house." I turned and walked away from Jalen without looking back. With each step, I felt vindicated and strong. I felt the revitalization that a new day brings; today represented the new me.

After my conversation with Jalen, I slept peacefully. My husband's hands rubbing my back awakened me. He whispered in my ear as he caressed my back. As Jalen touched me, I began to remember the loving times that my husband and I had shared. I remembered our first dance at the reception and how he sang in my ear. I remembered our honeymoon and how he made it worth all the time that I waited to share my body with a man. I remembered him holding my hand and wiping my forehead as I gave birth to Kylen. Was I wrong in roasting him about Alex? Should I really be concerned about her when I was the one who he comes home to? As I began to long for those times again, my body responded to the urge and I kissed my husband back. It was the first kiss that we had shared in months. Everything inside of me told me that I was kissing a stranger yet there was nothing strange about his touch. He ran his fingers through my hair as he kissed me with his lips slightly parted. Just as the moment between us began familiar, the phone rang. He begged me not to answer the phone, but a sense of urgency rang out with every ring of it. I rolled over, brushed my hair out of my face with my fingers and answered the phone, "Hello?"

"Hey Mel. Where is Jalen?"

"Sean? He's right here. Is everything okay?"

"Naw Mel. The ambulance just came and took Auntie to the hospital. She is really sick. Put J on the phone." I handed Jalen the phone and sat helplessly as he received the news that would rock his world. It was one thing to know that Ma was sick, but it was another to see that she was sick. I knew that he would need me and I would need him as well. Jalen hung up the phone, immediately climbed out of bed, and began to dress. I climbed out of bed right behind him and began to dress as quickly as possible.

As I dressed, Jalen looked at me out of the corner of his eye and grabbed his keys. "Mel, I need you to stay here with Kylen. It is too late for him to be out."

"Jalen, I am going to call the sitter for Kylen. I will meet you at the hospital. Which one did they take her to?"

"She was airlifted to Baptist Central." Jalen appeared to be annoyed at my insistence. "Mel, this is something that I need to take care of alone. This is a family thing—just stay here and I'll call you with an update." As Jalen spoke, I stopped lacing up the tennis shoe that I was working on and looked up at him in shock. He leaned over and kissed me quickly on the cheek as he ran out the door.

The first few moments after Jalen left, felt like an eternity in space. Time didn't exist, emotion didn't exist—there only existed a gap in sensibility. I was unable to make any sense of his actions. He went from kissing me and proclaiming love for me to leaving me here holding the pain of his abandonment. It wasn't just his mother that was ill, it was the only mother that I had known for sometime—yet it was a family thing. I went from being his wife and his heart to being less than family in a matter of moments. Foolishness flooded my mind and fell down my cheeks in liquid form.

I looked down at the 3-carat diamond ring that occupied my finger and twisted it. It slipped off of my finger very easily and fell to the floor. I watched as it rolled across the floor on its side and stopped right in front of the nightstand. Symbolically speaking, the ring meant the same in its current position, as it did on my finger—nothing. I was merely a placeholder for Jalen; I completed a perfect picture for the world to see. In the times that counted, Jalen always let me know where I stood. I decided at that moment that I would no longer place my happiness in his hands. I would bide my time, love me, and continue to take care of my family. This thing with Jalen would pass—as did everything else. Tears flowed from my eyes for another hour as I grieved the loss of my marriage and prepared for the new life that I was about to step into.

"Mama," Kylen's voice came with the sunrise the following morning. Blinking a few times to loosen up the dried tears that seemed to stick to my eyelashes, I greeted my son with a smile. "Hey baby," I spoke with my groggy morning voice. "Give mama a hug." Kylen climbed into my bed and gave me a sloppy kiss right on my eyelid. Turning the television on to his favorite cartoons, I lay in the bed with Kylen and rubbed the top of his head while he stared at the screen.

After about an hour or so of television, Jalen came into the room. He was wearing the same clothes that he had on last night when he left going to the hospital. He walked up to me, kissed me on the cheek, and set my wedding ring on top of the duvet'. "You must have dropped this Mel."

"No, I didn't drop it Jalen. I took it off. Thanks though." I rolled my eyes as I twisted the ring back onto my finger. "How's Ma? Or should I call her Mrs. Starks since I am not family now."

"Mel she is fine. Thanks for asking. And you would think that right now you would think a little less about your own sorry selfish pettiness and a little more about what I am going through. My mama is dying. I am sorry for not including you but I panicked last night. If it helps though, I missed having you there with me, and when she woke up, Ma asked about you too. Now if it's okay with you—I really need to go to bed. I was at the hospital all night and I am beat." Jalen plopped down in the bed next to Kylen and went straight to sleep without waiting to hear my response.

After Jalen fell asleep, Kylen and I went to the hospital to check on Ma. It was a very nice suite that she was in and I was right in the middle of braiding her hair when she began to speak. "Baby, I was looking for you this morning with Jalen. Him and Victor said that you weren't feeling all that well. Are you feeling any better now?"

"Yeah Mama, I am fine." I replied with all of the cheer that I could muster up. Jalen had brought Victor to the hospital and he definitely wasn't family. That was a huge slap in my face. I know that Victor is his best friend and maybe he needed some support. However, the fact that he chose to take him over me let me know that it wasn't that I didn't need to be here this morning. It was that he didn't want me here.

As I finished up Mama's hair, she talked constantly switching from subject to subject. "Girl I bet Jalen is at home sleeping. He didn't leave this hospital until about five am. That is my baby—he is a sweet child. I hope that lunch is a lot better than breakfast was. That breakfast was just awful."

"Ma, what time did you say that Jalen left?"

"About 5. Didn't you see him this morning before you left the house?"

"Yes Ma'am I saw him." I kept up with Mama's conversation though my mind was elsewhere. Jalen told me that he had just left the hospital this morning when he came in. That was about 8:30 or so. The hospital is only fifteen minutes from our home. So it was obvious that he and Victor made some other stops this morning. As I tried to sort things out in my head, Mama interrupted my thoughts with her conversation. "Mel, you should run and get Mama something to eat. Leave Kylen here with me. He'll be alright. I just can't stomach another nasty meal today."

"Yes Ma'am. What do you want to eat?"

"I want a Big Mac with extra sauce."

"Ma you are a little too old to be eating McDonald's. You need to eat something healthy. How about a chicken sandwich?" I laughed as I talked to Mama. She was a stubborn lady.

"No baby. I want a Big Mac. Don't make me call and get Jalen to bring it. Mama don't ask ya'll for much."

"Okay you can have it this time but next time you will be eating healthy. And don't be threatening me with Jalen. He sure wouldn't want you to have a Big Mac either." I grabbed my keys and walked out the door. As I walked, I felt a sharp pain in my stomach. The pain was so intense that it took the wind from me and made me crouch over holding my side. I sat still until the pain passed minutes later. Though I had shooting pains in my pregnancy with Kylen, they never rendered me unable to move. The intensity of the pain worried me, mentally I made a note to contact my doctor about the episode. As soon as I felt comfortable in my ability to move without pain, I picked up my purse and made my way to the car. Once in the car, I called my OB-GYN and made an appointment.

The scent of the Big Mac was not agreeing with my stomach. I drove hurriedly back to the hospital and rode up and down the rows of the parking lot looking for an available space. My heart skipped a beat when I spotted Alex's red Infiniti occupying one of the spaces. I was certain that it was her car because of the very vain license plate that her car had. On the plate, printed in big red letters was ICUJ. It read as: I see you J. There were two ways that this plate could be interpreted. It could be I see you are jealous. Or it could be I see you J as in Jalen. All of Jalen's acquaintances called him J, so why wouldn't his mistress call him that as well. I sighed deeply as I pulled into the parking space that was available only a couple of feet from Alex's and quickly grabbed my things. I wanted to catch her here and for once get to the bottom of things.

Rushing and breathing deeply, I charged into Mama's room looking wildly around for Alex. In my haste I tripped over one of Kylen's toys and dropped everything that I was holding in my hands. Mama looked up at me surprisingly and said, "Where's the fire?'

"No fire, Ma. I just didn't want to keep you waiting on this food." I looked around the room as I spoke and realized that Alex was not there. She must have been visiting someone else. "Ma did you have company while I was gone?"

"Honey ain't nobody been in here but one of the nurses and dietary. They came and brought me this dry plate of food. I told them they could keep it." As she spoke, I realized that my infatuation with the Alex thing was truly taking a toll on me. The stress alone was causing me to become ill and act with paranoia. I looked out in the hallway one more time and then decided to let the whole thing go. As long as she wasn't where I was, Alex would no longer be a concern of mine.

I made it a point to visit Mama every day. A month had passed and she was still there at the hospital where doctors thought that she would probably spend the remainder of her life. Jalen and I never visited her at the same time. It's as if, the stress of our marriage added to the stress of watching his mother live out her very last moments created a gap between us that could not be bridged with insincere terms of endearment. We communicated about a limited number of things: the baby, Kylen, the bills, and mama. There was never any loving conversation about us. He never asked how my day had been. Neither did I question him about his well being. It was as if we were two strangers sharing a life together.

The pregnancy progressed, though not without problems. I had a mild case of placenta previa that caused me to have episodes of intense pain. A cesarean section was scheduled for one month away and my mind was constantly whirling with concerns. Would Mama make it to meet the new baby? Would the baby be healthy? Today, however was a big day for our family and I made every attempt to get my mind off of the problems in my life.

The Minority Business Association of Virginia had selected Jalen as Businessman of the Year. It was a very auspicious occasion and I wanted to be certain not to ruin it for Jalen or me. In an attempt to look extra special for Jalen tonight, I bought a beautiful new dress and made plans with Kaiya to get an extra special hairstyle.

As I sat under the dryer at Kaiya's shop, I listened to some of the banter that surrounded me. I picked the conversation that sounded the juiciest and zeroed in on it. Anton, one of the stylists who rented a booth in the shop, was complaining about his new lover. It seems that this Tory guy that he was dating was increasingly unavailable. When Anton asked my opinion on the situation, I shifted uncomfortably. I was unable to give advice on this subject because I hadn't been intimate or spent time with my own husband in some time now. I had managed over time to maintain a picture perfect image and at this moment I was still unable to let anyone in on the truth about my home life. I smiled at Anton, and replied, "Boyfriend, you been working these men for years now. You know what you need to do. As a matter of fact, I could learn a few things from you." I gave the girl next to me a high-five and finished it off with a "You hear me." It was the perfect front to hide the fact that I too was having problems with my man. As Anton finished this subject and migrated to a new one, I quietly retreated into my own world behind a magazine.

Ky combed through my hair and complained about all of the fuss that I was going through for Jalen. "Girl he probably won't even notice all of this."

"Kaiya Yvette you know you need to be minding your business."

"Mel, I am only telling the truth. I don't want you to be disappointed tonight. Jalen is selfish, and you are too good to him. Here take this mirror and tell what you think." As Kaiya spoke, I checked my reflection in the mirror. Kaiya may not have wanted me to go through all of this but she made me look beautiful for the occasion. I handed her back the mirror and began to thank her for the advice and even more so for the hairstyle. "Ky, you have done it again. I love my hair. Thanks so much for taking care of me. Oh and don't worry about me—I am taking care of me. Remember what I said. I am just biding my time and taking care of my family. I gotta go and get me and Kylen dressed. Love ya." I handed Kaiya some money and quickly shuffled out the shop. On my way out, I gave Anton two "work it snaps" and blew him a kiss. If only he knew just how well I understood his pain.

The limousine pulled up at 5:00 on the dot. Jalen escorted Kylen and me out to the limo and much to my surprise Victor hopped out. Maybe this was his way of making sure that he didn't have to spend an awkwardly silent ride to the banquet. Or maybe he just wanted to share this very special occasion with his very best friend. Either way, I too was happy to see Victor—he always made sure that his baby sister was comfortable. I slid into the limousine seat directly across from Victor and watched as Jalen buckled Kylen's car seat into the seat next to me. After getting Kylen secure, Jalen slid into the seat on the other side of me and held my hand.

We rode in silence the whole way to the banquet. Victor would usually keep the conversation going, however this evening he seemed to have some things on his mind. He was quiet and reserved. Jalen held my hand the whole way and even whispered in my ear that I looked stunning. I thanked him shyly and nervously smoothed my hair out as we rode. I looked down at my selected attire and quietly celebrated its successful turnout. I chose a peach floor-length empire style evening gown with a plunging neckline. It wrapped around at the waist and tied on the side just above my belly with a satin sash that was trimmed with rhinestones. I was in my third trimester of pregnancy so it was very difficult to find a dress that fit the way that I wanted it to fit. Kaiya had given me very loose curls that were elegantly swept to one side of my head. I wore diamond chandelier earrings, a diamond tennis bracelet, and a 2 carat diamond pendant—all apology gifts given to me by Jalen during my first pregnancy.

Jalen wore a black Armani tuxedo. His tie was black with very thin peach pinstripes accessorized with diamond cufflinks and a diamond tie-pin. He smelled manly yet sexy and sported a fresh haircut. He literally looked like a million bucks. As we rode, I thought about Mama. She was so proud of Jalen and his accomplishments and had given me a card to give him right before the banquet. I took the card out of my tiny purse and handed it to my husband. As he read it tears slowly fell from his eyes. Though no words were spoken, this was the first time that he and I had communicated emotionally in months. At that moment I began to expect it to be a great night, a night of accomplishment for my husband and a night of love for us.

"And without further ado, I present our man of the evening, Dr. Jalen Starks. Please stand and receive him." The crowd stood to its feet and began to applaud as Jalen made his way to the podium. He walked proud and confidently and nodded his head in acknowledgment as he thanked the crowd for the applause. He paused for one moment, looked over at our table, which was occupied by Kylen, Victor, Mrs. Anne, and myself, and began to speak. "Thank you so much for this wonderful honor. The Minority Business Association is a huge pillar in our community and I am so honored to have been chosen by them for such a special reward. While, some consider my family practice to be a business, I consider it to be an opportunity to affect change and to help my fellow brother. Others consider catering to be a successful business but as I see it—people gotta eat." He paused as people laughed at his joke, cleared his throat and continued. "I would like to thank a few people for supporting me so far. To all of the employees of the Starks Family Practice and A Touch of Class Catering, I would like to say thank you. To my father posthumously, I hope you are proud. I would like to thank my mother who is in the hospital right now fighting cancer. Mama you are the reason that I am who I am. To my son Kylen and to the baby on the way—Daddy loves you. Finally, I want to thank the cornerstone of support, the person who has been there for me through it all, and pushed me to be the best that I can be. To my very best friend in the world, Victor, thank you from the bottom of my heart. Again thanks to the MBA and may you all have much continued success to come."

As Jalen made his way back to his seat, my palms began to sweat, my heart pounded, and tears welled up in my eyes. I wanted so badly to run out of the room in shame. I could feel the blood rush to my face and ears as it normally does when I am flustered. Jalen did not even mention me in his speech. It was my catering business that I started long before he ever came along that he was being recognized for. I was his wife and he didn't even mention my name. He thanked my employees, and my kids, but didn't thank me. I felt cheated, neglected, abused, and most of all pissed off. He even mentioned Victor, which wasn't a surprise to me. How did he forget his own wife. I felt the eyes in the room staring at me; every woman in the room knew what I was feeling. The embarrassment grew as Jalen got closer to the table and began shaking hands in the area. Victor reached across the table, touched my hand, and signaled me to keep my head up. I responded by taking a deep breath, holding my head up and my shoulders back. As Jalen sat down at the table he looked at me and immediately realized that he did not even mention my name. Remorse clouded his face as I glared at him and began to nervously twist my wedding ring. He leaned over and kissed me softly and slowly on the lips while the flashes of cameras went off all around us in slow motion. In some feeble attempt to fix the situation, he stroked my cheek and mouthed the words thank you to me. As he did this some of the stares in the room softened as if they were sold by his actions. I was not convinced however. When it counted—he did not mention me and no underhanded tactics would hide the truth of what had just happened.

    I sat the rest of the banquet in complete silence. I did not applaud, I did not smile, and I certainly did not acknowledge the man that sat next to me. He was a ghost of my past, no longer the husband that I knew and loved. As we rode in the limousine, I rubbed Kylen's cheek as he fell asleep. It had been a long day for him and an even longer and more tiresome day for me. Jalen made no attempt to reconcile with me. Perhaps he knew that this mistake was one that could not be fixed with one of his, "Baby I need you" lines. Jalen and Victor celebrated the entire trip home. They both made pacts that next year's Man of the Year" would be Victor Laines, Attorney at Law.

The car could not pull up to our door quick enough. I felt as if I was suffocating in anger. I was out of the car and barging through my front door seemingly before the limo came to a complete stop. I had to get away from Jalen before I could no longer hold the tears. I had to escape the charade that he and Victor put on in the car. There was no consideration of my feelings, I knew this and could not deal with the reality of it. I turned the key and ran through the house straight up the stairs and directly to my bathroom. Once in the bathroom, I began to release the rage that was pinned up inside of me for the past year. I kicked my shoes off and threw one of them into the mirror causing it to crack. I began to swing my fist at the air with all of the force that I could muster. Tears poured from my eyes and profanities flew from my mouth. I cursed Jalen, I cursed Alex, and I cursed my self for the fool that I had been for both of them. I was a puppet in the shape of a wife whose actions were controlled by the strings that Jalen had been pulling since he and I met.

I began to pull at my hair as the resentment grew. I always wore hairstyles that Jalen loved and had actually forgotten what my own sense of style was prior to him coming into my life. I violently removed the dress that I was wearing. While it was a beautiful dress, it was not what I would have considered my style. It was Jalen's style. As I raged on in this little space, I began to tire. I fell to my knees and allowed the emotion that I was feeling to overcome me. I released every inch of the woman that Jalen had created and molded into being his fool of a wife.

Finally, when the hurt was too much, the rage passed. I sat on both knees in the floor of my bathroom. There were mirrors on every wall however I could not bring myself to look in one. I could not face the person that I had become. "Mama, don't cry." I slowly raised my head to see Kylen standing in front of me. He wiped my eyes and smiled saying, "I love you, Mama." I took Kylen in my arms and held him there. As I hugged him, I felt myself gaining strength. Without letting him go, I stood to my feet and faced myself in the mirror. I took a long look at the face that it reflected and vowed to search for the person that used to stare back at me in the mirror. Starting today, I would find, like, and love Melany Starks.

By the time I tucked Kylen into bed, I was mentally drained from the evening. Of course, Jalen wasted no time before going out with Victor. He didn't even get out of the limo—he simply unbuckled Kylen and sent him into the house after me. I found relief in the silence of the house; it was peaceful and the opposite of the raging war that existed within my marriage. I was actually very grateful that Jalen was not home. I plopped into bed, adjusted the sheets, and snuggled my face into my down pillows. Immediately after I found the comfortable spot for the night, the phone rang. I sighed as I clicked on the lamp and checked the caller id. It was Ky. "Ky—do you know what time it is? You are only calling to be nosy. You know this could have waited until morning." I yawned constantly as I spoke. "What do you want?"

"Mel," Kaiya was talking with plenty of energy. "One of my customers went to the banquet and girl she just called me and told me that Jalen straight clowned you. Honey she said that he thanked everybody and they momma but didn't even mention you. Mel, please tell me that she is lying. I know you didn't get all dressed up and cute to have him show out like that in front of all of Virginia. Am I gone have to cut Jalen?"

"Ky," I didn't want to excite her any further so I thought carefully before I spoke. "I am so tired. I will have to call you tomorrow and tell you everything. But I want you to know that I am okay. I will call you as soon as I wake up. Love ya." I hung up the phone without waiting on Kaiya to say good-bye. I certainly did not want to be rude, however at that exact moment what I needed was some rest and some alone time. I knew she would understand. I started my getting comfortable process all over and before long found peace in a night of sound sleep.

Chapter 6

▼

Weeks had passed and the sting of Jalen's betrayal at his honoree banquet had yet to go away. It was surprising just how many people were there on that night and bared witness to my shame. I had employees from my catering business, nurses from Jalen's office, girlfriends from around the way, and even people I passed on the street trying to console me. It seemed that every pat on the back caused me to relive the moment and the rage within me to build again.

I was scheduled to give birth to our new baby in just two short weeks. We had no idea what sex it would be because it was uncooperative in the sonograms that we were given to determine the gender of the baby. Jalen said the whole time that he knew it would be a little princess and had already come up with a name for her. It would be Kaylen Victoria Starks. The first name was very similar to Kylen, which consisted of Kaiya and Jalen's names blended. The middle name, Victoria, was taken from Victor of course. It seemed only right to do this because Victor was the godfather of Kylen and the expected baby. If it happened to be a boy, his name would be Keelan. I would be happy at either outcome, but I already had a boy so my bias was secretly leaning towards a girl.

I sat on the floor in the nursery and smiled as I folded the blankets, bibs, and booties that I had received as gifts for the baby. Everything in the room was pure white. It had an angelic theme and was truly fit for my little angel that was on the way. I carefully arranged the baby's lotion, shampoo, powder, oil, and diapers; taking a moment to relax and enjoy the silence in the room. This was the most peaceful room in the house and while I was actually doing work in the room—it was there that I felt the most relaxed. Jalen calling out to me from our bedroom interrupted my peace. "Mel—hey Melany. Come here."

"Can't you come in here Jalen? It was hard enough for me to get down here. Now you want me to get up." I sighed as I mumbled under my breath, "A please would have been nice." I rocked back and forth on my bottom until I gained the momentum to get to my feet. Every step that I made towards the bedroom sent sharp pains through my swollen feet. "What is it Jalen?"

"Where is my gray tie with the blue stripes? I can't find the shoes that I wear with this suite either?" He pointed to a suit that was on a pile of clothes laying across the bed. His luggage bag was nearby and his packing was almost complete. Jalen was packing for another so-called convention. He had given me a huge 48-hour notice of this 2-day trip. However, I was certain that it was just another rendezvous with Alex. It was my goal to get his lying butt packed and out of the house as quickly as possible. I didn't care where he went at this point. In my mind, we were only married on paper anyway.

I looked forward to every chance that I got to be at home without Jalen. The stress in the house was removed when he left, and Kylen and I always had a ball. I rummaged through the closet and found them both in very obvious places and placed them on the bed next to his luggage bag. I made sure to show my irritation. "Anything else Jalen?" I asked in a very dry tone. This was what our communication had come to—very short and to the point sentences.

Jalen looked up at me and quickly looked back down as he continued to pack. "Uhh, I need q-tips, Vaseline, toothpaste, and my toothbrush. That is—if you don't mind."

"I don't mind…" I said as I walked off. "As long as it gets you outta here quicker." I mumbled under my breath. Though he couldn't hear me—I secretly got satisfaction from having sarcastic retorts. After handing him every item that he needed, I shuffled back down to the nursery to resume the organizing.

About twenty minutes later, I heard the front door close and the rumble of Jalen driving away. He did not say good-bye and it didn't matter to me one bit. I felt that the fewer words that we exchanged— the better. I checked the clock, and realized that Kylen would be home shortly and would want a snack as usual. I finished things up in the nursery, rose to my feet, and headed to the kitchen.

I prepared Kylen's favorite snack of peanut butter and applesauce, until I began to feel cramps in my stomach. I quickly put his plate on the counter and sat on the barstool to my right. I was seriously stressed and naturally assumed that rest would help me feel better. Knowing that I would need some help with Kylen, I went and grabbed the cordless phone and gave Kaiya a call.

She answered before I said a word, "Sup Mel."

"Hey Ky. You need to come and stay here tonight. I'm tired and I need to lie down but Kylen will be here in a minute. Girl you know he won't let me have any rest once he gets here. How many heads do you have left?"

"Honey I ain't doin' no hair right now. I am out looking at shoes. I'm going by my house to pick up a few things. I'll see you in a minute."

"Okay," I replied between my teeth as the intensified pain came again. Shortly before my hand reached the end button, I heard Kaiya call my name again. I put the phone back to my ear, "Huh Ky?"

"I am going to pick up a pizza for dinner. So you just get off them big ole' feet and get in the bed." As Kaiya hung up, I looked down at my feet and laughed to myself. Kaiya had always had much bigger feet than I did and she loved the fact that she could finally call me "big feet" now that mine were severely bloated.

Kaiya arrived a long and painful 45 minutes after our conversation, with Kylen in her arms. I was immediately greeted by his big smile as he handed me a scribbled drawing on red construction paper. I hugged Kylen as if I hadn't seen him in days. The pain that radiated down my spine burned clear to my knees, causing me to struggle to hold Kylen as I braced myself on a chair with one free hand. My scream alerted Kaiya; she jumped into action and grabbed Kylen from my arms. When the moment passed, I realized that Kaiya had taken Kylen out of the room. She was standing by my side holding me around my waist with one hand and holding my hair off of my sweating neck with the other. I straightened up and began to walk into the den, before Kaiya stopped me in my tracks. "Melany, are you in labor? Girl you better not be in labor. I am not equipped to handle that type of stuff."

"Naw girl. Ain't nobody in labor, I am just having a few pregnancy pains, that's all. If I were in labor, you'd know it—believe me."

"Okay," Kaiya spoke with her eyebrows raised in doubt. "Let me know if you need me to take you to the hospital. Anyway, are you ready to eat? I got us a veggie pizza."

"Yeah. Let me go get Kylen so he can eat too?" I headed to Kylen's room, sliding my feet across the floor as I walked. Kylen was lying in his race car bed with his feet propped up against the wall, watching his favorite cartoons. "Hey Mama," Kylen greeted me as if he hadn't seen me five minutes earlier. He turned, placed both feet on the floor and ran to me, saying, "Eat."

"Yeah baby. Let's go downstairs so we can eat." Kylen ran ahead of me and sat down on the top stair. I had taught him to scoot down the stairs on his bottom because Kylen still had stumpy legs that were too short to conquer the steps upright. I began to feel a warm stream running down my leg with each step I took. Initially I assumed that I might have had an "embarrassing leak". I called out to Kaiya to watch Kylen as I went to the restroom, and made my way back up the stairs. I turned and retraced my steps back up the stairs, and began to panic. There were drops of blood on each step and a small puddle on the step that I was standing on. Carefully, I hurried up the steps and to my bathroom. Grabbing a hand mirror, I inspected myself to see what was actually going on below.

While I held the mirror, it quickly became covered in blood affecting my ability to see anything. My breath escaped me and I began to gasp for air. Pushing the intercom button repeatedly, I called out to Kaiya in the kitchen. "Ky, get Kylen's overnight bag and meet me downstairs in three minutes, it should already be packed and in his closet. Oh and keep Kylen down there with you please."

"Are you okay?"

"Yeah I am fine. I just found b-l-o-o-d." I spelled it out to keep Kylen from worrying. "I will be down in a minute. Wrap him up some pizza to go."

"Okay." Kaiya's voice quaked. We were both freaking out. I quickly changed into a jogging suit and protected myself from the mess. With my pre-packed overnight back in one hand and the banister in the other, I took each step slowly. When I finally made it to the foyer, Kaiya was there with my son in her arms. She was holding the front door wide open for me and breathing hard. Kaiya squinted her eyes and said, "Didn't I tell you that I can't handle this type of stuff?"

"You think I be listening to you." I said mocking her. "I don't be listening to you." I leaned over and kissed my best friend on the cheek as I walked past her out the door. Using a towel to protect her seats, I climbed into Kaiya's Lexus SUV and gripped the door handle in pain. She buckled Kylen in and jumped into the front seat. With the world in a blur, we sped to the hospital.

When we pulled into the circular driveway of the Women's Hospital, the seriousness of my situation began to take its toll on me. Every turn that we made produced gut-wrenching pain. Kylen sat behind me completely oblivious to what was going on with Mommy in the front seat. Kaiya threw the gear into park and hopped out of the SUV. She ran into the hospital and emerged only seconds later with an employee pushing a wheelchair. The wheelchair squeaked under my weight, causing the hair on the back of my neck to stand up. I had to contact Jalen. He had no idea that his baby and I were in trouble. He had to get here. "Wait, wait. I need to call my husband. I can't do this without him being here."

"Mel, I will call Jalen, but right now we have to get you inside so someone can look at you. That baby may be in danger." Kaiya got her cell phone out of her purse and handed it to me as they began to roll me away. The nurse then held her hand out as if to let me know that I could not take the phone with me. "Ma'am" the nurse said with a sugary southern drawl, "no cell phones are aloud in admissions. You will have to leave the cell phone with her."

"Okay," my voice shook while I tried to remain calm. "When can she and my son join me?"

"Well, she can join you in about fifteen minutes, but we don't usually allow kids as young as he is in the back. The experience can be too traumatic for young eyes." The nurse was trying to be as diplomatic as possible with her comments. She must have seen the emotion in my eyes. I was spewing with desperation. She softened her gaze, shrugged her shoulders and whispered, "I really am sorry, ma'am."

"Sorry, no sweetheart, sorry is not going to get it. You don't tell a woman who pays good money to be here that she can't bring her child with her. Your saying that it might traumatize him—can you imagine how traumatized he would be if I left him in the car? Kaiya is my support system because my husband, DR. JALEN STARKS, is away at a Physician's Convention. So I don't care who you have to go ask—but somebody needs to make arrangements for my son to come with me until his sitter is able to get here to pick him up. Am I clear?" By this time I was yelling at the nurse. It took everything I had not to allow profanities to fly from my mouth and my hands to go around her neck. I was hurting intensely, bleeding profusely, and in danger of losing my unborn child and this nurse had me in the lobby talking about my son. The anger and pain grew in a parallel nature and between the two my head began to spin. My outburst had obviously upset my son, as his lip began to quiver. I took Kylen by his hand, leaned over and whispered, "Mama is just fine baby. I love you." As my voice trailed off, so did my consciousness.

Stars danced before my eyes, and a zoom sound rang in my ears as I came to. I was lying in a hospital bed, with an oxygen mask covering my mouth and nose. My throat was dry as cotton, and my fingertips and toes tingled. I slowly looked around the room and saw Kaiya to my right. She had tears running down her eyeliner-smeared face. When her gaze met mine she breathed a huge sigh of relief and began to run her fingers through my hair. Immediately I began to cry, first quietly and softly. Kylen was not in Kaiya's lap and panic began to run down my spine making me shudder. My mouth dropped as I noticed the curtain that covered me from my stomach down.

Suddenly the doctors and nurses that occupied the room emerged from the blur. I was having a c-section.

"No, please. I can't have my baby yet. Not without Jalen. Kaiya, please tell them to wait just a little longer." I wanted to kick and scream but I had no feeling in my extremities. A huge wave of sorrow came over me as I realized that I would have my child without Jalen. The doctors had to work quickly to free my child from my womb before it became a tomb. As I cried, Kaiya sat quietly, and stroked my cheek. She knew that there were no words that could comfort me. Closing my eyes, I secretly surrendered my life in hopes that it would save my baby.

"I'm almost done." The voice of one of the doctors put me on alert for the news of my child. I stared at the white ceiling and squinted at the bright lights in the room. I looked down and began to study the sheet that separated me from the surgery that was taking place below. It was cotton, with blue stripes. I began to count the stripes—not in a fully sound state of mind. "One, two, three…"

"We have a big baby girl." I looked down and saw my doctor standing with Kaylen Victoria Starks in his hands. "We have to go ahead and quickly get her to NICU for testing and stabilizing. That is just to make sure that she is okay. This was a very traumatic delivery and it is policy after emergency c-sections to send the baby for further observation. However, she looks fine and she should start crying about now." Just as he said that, Kaylen let out her first very loud scream. The more that the nurses worked on her the more she screamed. It was music to my ears. One of the nurses brought her over to Kaiya and me. I watched as Kaiya held her a short second and then put her up next to my face. I kissed my little girl and one of my tears dropped on her pale cheek. Her tears immediately stopped and she peered at me through squinted eyes. She was beautiful.

Within seconds, the nurses placed Kaylen in a warm incubator and rolled her out of the room. With my little girl gone, I began to feel dizzy and nauseated. The stripes on the curtain were no longer in a straight line. They now appeared to be squiggly lines that moved. The room spun and my chest became very heavy. I struggled to catch my breath as I looked at Kaiya. Her face read fear and she too began to cry. I watched Kaiya as she began to fade into black. "She's losing too much blood!" The doctors were yelling at the nurses for help. They too faded away.

I awoke to Jalen sitting in a chair staring at me. He had his hands together in his lap with his fingers interwoven. As soon as he realized that I was awake, he jumped out of his seat and ran to my bedside. "Oh my God Mel! You scared us so bad. Baby I love you so much. I just knew that I was going to lose you. The doctors said that if you didn't wake up in the next few hours, they would begin to worry." He kissed me repeatedly on my forehead and cheek—but did not touch my lips. "Oh sweetheart, Victoria is so beautiful. She looks just like you. I can't believe she came so early. I know she didn't get that from you. You are always late."

As Jalen spoke, I stared at his mouth moving rapidly. Nervous chatter continuously flowed from his mouth and every word disgusted me. What man would go away with his lover for two days with his wife being two weeks away from delivering their child? What kind of jerk would pull some mess like that? My belly ached from the surgery, and my memory was still cloudy about the preceding events. My head was spinning from the blood that I had lost, and still through all of that—I hated my husband. I wanted him to leave my room. I wanted him to exit my life, and free me from the bondage of being a wife to this ungrateful and sorry excuse of a man. Deep hatred bubbled within me and was seconds away from spewing from my mouth. I paused when I saw Kaylen Victoria Starks in her bassinet in the corner of the room. "How much did she weigh, Ky?" Kaiya sat up from the makeshift bed and answered me before Jalen could get any words out. "She was 9 pounds 3 ounces, and 21 inches long."

"No wonder she tore my insides up. I'm a petite little thing and here she come weighing nine pounds." I laughed as I spoke. With each shake of my body, the seams of my incision burned making me hold my belly. "Girl, what happened to me? I don't remember a thing."

"Baby, your previa turned serious and ruptured. You lost quite a bit of blood." Jalen had spoken up as if he was jealous of the fact that I was asking Kaiya about my medical state. "They had to get Victoria out of you to save her life."

"First of all", I interrupted Victor. "I was talking to Kaiya. She is the one who was here with me. Everything you are saying is stuff you were told after the fact." I rolled my eyes away from Jalen and directed my attention back to Kaiya, "as I was saying, Ky what happened?"

"Well everything that he said is correct. However, after Kaylen was born though, you began to bleed really badly and you lost consciousness. You have been out for about two days." As Kaiya spoke, Jalen looked down at his feet and pretended to kick at something that was on the floor. "Mel", Kaiya paused. "You nearly died."

"Almost died?" I repeated Kaiya's last two words hoping that they wouldn't be true the next time. I looked at Jalen with a glare that could melt steel. He mouthed "I'm sorry" to me and dropped his head in shame. I knew there wasn't a convention in the first place. He had taken Alex out of town and I knew it. I held my stare on him, conveying some of the anger with my eyes. The room began to warm up and my stomach turned flips. I felt my mouth watering and knew that I was about to be sick. Just in time, I leaned over into the garbage and threw up all of my frustrations and anger. Jalen ran around the bed to where I sat, and placed a cold towel on my neck. He held my hair while he rubbed my back in a circular motion.

Just as I began to feel a little better, I jerked my head away from his touch. "Kaiya bring Kaylen to me, please. Let me hold my little Princess." She put Kaylen in my arms and my heart softened. She was beautiful. She had lots of jet-black hair with curls about the diameter of a straw. Her legs were long and her wrinkled skin was a pale pinkish-peach color. I looked into her eyes in awe of the lakes of beauty in them. When I rubbed her soft tiny hand, she wrapped her fingers tightly around my index finger. Looking into my baby's face was like peering at a mirror—only I saw more peace in her than I had ever seen in me. She yawned and gently fell asleep in my arms.

Kaylen had been asleep for about 30 minutes or so and still I gazed at her, careful to take in every magnificent detail. Jalen came and stood behind me adoring our baby over my shoulder. I adjusted her little pink hat, pulled her t-shirt down and handed her to Jalen. Our eyes met when he reached out to get her, "Mel, I should have been here. I should have remembered to call your name at the banquet. I should have been a better husband to you and a much better father to our kids. You don't have to answer me now—but please know…", he seemed to be choked up as he spoke. "Please know that I am truly sorry. I don't know what my world would be like without you. You have given me two beautiful kids and all I have given you is hell. Things will change today—right now, I promise."

As Jalen, spoke I watched Kaiya from over his shoulder signaling to me. She mimicked a cutting motion across her neck as to say, "Kill that noise" and motioned her hand in the "Blah, blah, blah fashion." I realized that Jalen was done speaking and I slowly turned my attention to him. "Where is Kylen?"

"She's with Reece."

"Jalen, go pick him up and bring him up here, please. I miss my little man."

"Okay baby. Do you need me to get you anything else?"

"No Jalen, just my son." I was frustrated by his fake concern and his very lackadaisical approach at making things right. I just wanted him gone.

Jalen picked up his cell phone and walked over to kiss me good-bye. Just as his lips were about to make contact with my cheek I leaned away from him, scratched my head and waved him away. "Jalen just go get Kylen, okay?" Defeat clouded his face and Jalen slowly walked out of the room, never lifting his feet from the floor.

We listened for the bell of the elevator before Kaiya began to laugh. She hit her leg three times in amusement as she giggled. "Girl, you are finally giving that man a taste of his own medicine. Honey he looked like somebody had shot his dog. But I don't blame you—I would kill Mark if he left me here to have his baby all by myself."

"Well Ky", I talked as I adjusted my sheets. "I hope his night with Alex was worth it. They both make me sick. I can't stand that heifer."

"Don't you mean his two nights with Alex? Girl, he just got here last night."

"Last night? When did you call him? Didn't he know I was in labor?"

"Yes Mel." Kaiya dropped her head as she spoke. Perhaps she couldn't bear the pain that her next few statements were going to bring me. "I called Jay as soon as they rolled you into admissions. He didn't answer so I left a message on his voicemail. I called him about three more times before they took you in for the surgery. He finally returned my call right after Kaylen was born. I told him what the deal was and he said okay and hung up. Mel, he didn't show one bit of emotion—he just hung the phone up." Tears ran a familiar path down my face. I realized now that even when he knew that I was delivering the baby, dying, and alone—he still didn't come to the hospital until his trip was over. I looked at Kaiya, wiped my running nose, and picked up my new daughter. "At least now I know where we stand."

Chapter 7

The weeks following Victoria's birth had been rather tough. Because my surgery was very traumatic, I suffered a lot of pain in the time that followed and stayed in the hospital for a few weeks. The miracle lied in the fact that Victoria did not suffer one ailment from my troubled pregnancy. It was a true blessing that she came into this world in completely perfect health. I was able to convince Kaiya to spend the majority of her time with me at my house when I was finally discharged. While I was healing, she was there to help me get everyday tasks around the house complete. She also helped me to ignore Jalen.

The day that I came home from the hospital, Jalen again plotted out the perfect "apology". He arranged to have a welcome home spa for me. He had hired a masseuse, a chef, manicurist/pedicurist, and a sitter for the kids. He also had the bedroom completely redecorated with a new plasma television and a new bedroom suit that I had fallen in love with some months prior. Those gifts used to bandage the wounds that his betrayal left—now they seemed to salt them. It was as if he insulted my intelligence with half-hearted appeals to my insecurities. While I was aware of his ulterior motives behind the hired services, I did use each and every one of them without speaking one word to Jalen. He didn't even get a thank you.

As the days turned into weeks, Jalen quickly returned to his old self. His time at home shortened and his kind comments gradually began to waver. Victor also began to spend more time over at our house. He would run errands for me, play with Kylen and Kaylen, and keep Jalen out of my way. It was as if he knew that Jalen and I were living unfamiliar and separate lives together. Both Kaiya and Victor were my heroes, and they each became big parts of my family.

It had been a lazy day so far and Jalen had taken the kids to visit his mama at the hospital. I was lying on my brand new apology bed watching my apology television and picking the polish off of my apology manicure, when the phone rang. Kaiya was supposed to be coming over to do my hair so I assumed it was she. I answered the phone sweetly without even looking at the caller id, "Helloooo."

"Hey girl!" The voice that came through the line made my heart literally stop beating for about 10 seconds. I looked at the receiver in my hand with absolute astonishment. With no words, I softly placed the phone back on the receiver and went back to watching the television. Within seconds the phone rang again. Then it rang again. I watched as the phone rang three times before I got up the nerve to answer it. I picked up the phone, bit my lip, and yelled, "Hello?"

"Hey Mel, I think your phone is acting funny because it sounded like you hung up on me. Long time, no hear from."

"I know…", I made sure to speak with an attitude as I turned the volume down on the TV to ensure that heard correctly. "This better not be who I think it is."

"It depends on who you think it is."

"Look Alex. It's one thing to try to see me out in public, but to call my house. You are way out of line. I tell you what, you got…"

"Mel, you really need to pump your brakes. Ain't nobody callin' for you. Where is Jalen?" My mouth literally sat wide open. This tramp had the nerve to call my house and asked for my husband. Their affair was now becoming a blatant slap in my face. However, I knew that she was only doing this because I was incapacitated for the moment. Oh, but I had a trick for Miss Alex. The state I was in now was not permanent and she would definitely get hers. I could not show her my anger, I would not reveal my intimidation. I pursed my lips, looked up to the heavens and answered, "How did you get this number?"

"How you think I got it? Now put Jalen on the phone."

"Alex, don't call my house anymore. If you have business with Jalen, his office hours are from nine to five. Aside from that, you will not disrespect my home in this way again. This is my last warning, what happens from here is on you."

"Melany Starks", Alex said as she laughed hysterically. "Are you trying to threaten me? You really need to quit playin'. Ain't nobody scared of you. But for real, when Jalen gets home, he'll want to know that I called. So you should probably be sure to tell him. Bye Mel. Oh and kiss the baby for me." Alex blew a kiss into the phone before she hung up. The phone began to beep as I held it in my hand long after Alex had hung up.

It seemed that with every incident that passed, the level of disrespect between Alex and Jalen was growing. We were suddenly at the point where the sanctity of my home was being challenged. I had a job to do and that was to ensure that my kids grew up in a peaceful well-balanced home, and Alex was threatening that. I was left with no choice but to take care of this once and for all.

I needed to talk to Jalen about this relationship that we had ignored for so long. I reached for the phone to call him and it rang in my hand before I could dial. I guessed that Alex was calling back to taunt me a little more. I quickly answered the phone, "What the hell?"

"Mel!" It was Jalen and he was noticeably crying into the phone. "She's gone."

"Who's gone? What?"

"My Mama. Mel, she's gone." The news shattered the moment and minimized the incident that preceded it. Jalen continued to speak, sobbing uncontrollably into the phone, "I brought Kylen and Victoria up here and she seemed okay while she was visiting with them. I should have known that something was wrong because of how she stared at the kids and me. She also kept asking where you were and saying that she loved us. We were in the parking lot leaving the hospital when they called me back upstairs. Mel, by the time I got up there my mama was gone."

"No Jalen, they said that she had another month or so. What happened—what happened?" At this point I too was crying. This was not supposed to happen this way. I hadn't gotten to see Mama since before I had the baby. I needed to see her again. I needed to tell her that I loved her. "Jalen, come get me. Come get me now. I have to see her."

"Mel", Jalen yelled into the phone. "It's too late. She is gone. She wanted me to tell you that she loves you. She also got to hold Princess. That was the last thing she did before she passed." By that time, Jalen's tears had stopped and he seemed to be handling things a little better. "Mel, I am on the way home. I think we need each other right now."

I slowly hung the phone up. Alex's phone call was so unimportant to me and to my family now. My mind was in a whirlwind and I found myself unable to come to grips with losing Mama. I began to revisit the time that I lost my mother. I was only eighteen years old when she was killed by a drunk driver. My second semester at Virginia Tech had been kind of demanding. I would talk to her every single morning before my first class. It was as if she and I were long distance roommates. I was pledging that semester and it had been a really tough past few weeks.

On the morning of the day that she died, Mom had sent me tulips with a teddy bear. The note said "I can't bear being away from you." That was the first time that I had every received flowers and the cheesy bear and note meant the world to me. I called my Mom, thanked her, and complained a little more about pledging. We didn't talk long but I did tell her that I loved her and she told me that she loved me too. If I would have known that it was the last time we would speak—I would have said so much more. I would have told her that she was the best Mom that a girl could ask for. I would have thanked her for sacrificing so much for me. I would have told her just how happy she made me.

I was an only child, so I had to bury my Mom all by myself. At eighteen, I was forced to learn to live as an adult on my own. It was the toughest loneliest period of my life thus far. From there, I dropped line, dropped out of school, moved into her house and took over her catering business. Because I missed my mother so much, for years I lived a life of seclusion leaving the house only to work. That is until I met Jalen; he brought excitement to my life. He was the reason that I went back and finished school. He supported me in my catering business and actually referred several clients to me. With his help and support, it became of the largest in the city, and I learned how to live again.

The familiar pain of losing a mother began to sting in my chest as I snapped back into the painful present. Mama Starks fought cancer for over a year and had given it her best shot. I was torn between the grief of losing her and the closure of knowing that she was finally at peace. I stood up off of the floor and went into the bathroom. My eyes were swollen from crying and tear streaks had dried on my face. Slowly, I began to run me a warm bath. As the water ran—I sat on the edge of the tub and quietly let the tears fall into my lap.

The days after Mama passed were eerily peaceful in our home. We had visitors in and out, most of whom were Jalen's friends and family. He and I were leaning on each other for support and we seemed to have grown a little closer through it all.

I was the person in the family who took the initiative to make the funeral arrangements for Ma. Over the weeks when I visited her in the hospital, she gave me in depth instruction on how she wanted things to be done. Mama had even picked out what she wanted to be buried in from a magazine. Jalen was also an only child, so there really was no one else there to carry out her final wishes.

Jalen and I were lying on our bed with the "To Do" List in front of us. He childishly played with my hair while I looked through the funeral catalogue to find the perfect casket for Mama. When I found the one that she had described to me, I marked it down on the forms that the funeral director had given me. I sat up on the bed with my legs crossed and began to look through the list of obituary formats. As I turned the pages, Jalen reached out and put his hand on top of my right hand. He looked at me in my eyes for about five seconds, then reached out and moved a piece of hair out of my face with his index finger. He then traced his finger down the side of my face and neck all the way down to my cleavage. His timing was awkward, none of this was expected. I giggled at the tickling affect that it had on me. The more I giggled, the more he touched and tickled me. Before long, Jalen and I were rolling on the bed wrestling and tickling one another. He rolled me over on my back and straddled my stomach, tickling and kissing me on my neck. Suddenly, he paused with my arms pinned down and stared at my face. Next, he leaned in and kissed me softly. It was the same kiss that he gave me the first time he said I love you. It was the same kiss that he gave me the night he proposed. He also kissed me that same way when we shared our first dance as husband and wife. And now for the first time in years—I was being kissed again by a man who truly loved me.

When our lips finally parted, Jalen had one tear running down his face. I too was tearful by this point. He then touched my face and began to speak his heart to me. "Mel, you have been so good to me. Here you are taking care of my Mama's funeral. Her own sisters aren't even helping you. You truly are a remarkable woman. There are so many things that I wish I could undo. There are so many things that I want to share with you. You are a beautiful and special lady and your kindness speaks measures about your mother's kindness. She would be so proud of the woman that you have become—just like my mama was. Please know that no matter what happens from here—you should have and will always deserve the best."

"Jalen...", I was almost speechless. I reached out and ran my fingers across his lips. "Shhh—I know. That's all in the past now. We will live from here, from today...from now." We kissed again and

Jalen laid his head on my lap. As I stroked his wavy hair—I thought about every thing that we had been through as a couple. I looked up and smiled as I thought about Mama's advice, "No matter what Mel, take care of your marriage." At this moment, I was glad that I listened to her.

I managed to get almost all of the arrangements taken care of on my own. Jalen's aunt wrote the obituary out and brought it over so we could to take it to be printed. Jalen insisted on helping and took it to be printed up for me. The teamwork made it so that everything was taken care of in a very orderly fashion; just as mama had wanted. On one of our visits at the hospital she told me, "I don't want no mess thrown together for me. Ya'll better make my homegoing right. And make sure whoever cooks for the repass can cook. Ain't nothing worse than havin' nasty food after a funeral." I laughed as I thought about some of the crass things that she would say.

I stood in the mirror for about 30 minutes adjusting my black hat. The funeral was today and in all of my running around I didn't have the time to get my hair fixed. Maybe it was the nervousness of having to say good bye that made it so difficult for me to get myself dressed. Jalen was also having a tough time getting ready. He was nervously pacing the floor inside his closet trying to find something to wear. Kylen and Kaylen were with Kaiya, giving us more time to get ourselves prepared. I decided to give Jalen a hand at picking out his clothes to hopefully relieve some of the stress that I was sure he was feeling. I picked out a nice plain black suit and laid it out on the bed for him. Next, I laid out a white shirt; gray, light blue, and black striped tie; cufflinks; socks; and shoes. As I did this, Jalen watched me with tears in his eyes and quietly began to dress himself.

Jalen fumbled with his tie knot in frustration for about two minutes before falling to his knees in tears. "Mel, I can't do this. I can't go."

"Come on baby. You know your mama wouldn't have you being this upset. Jalen she only wanted you to be happy. You are her baby boy and we all need you to be strong." While I spoke to Jalen, I finished tying his tie for him and closed his cufflinks.

Within the hour, we were both dressed and ready to go. I stood behind Jalen in the mirror and admired his handsome qualities. He had smooth dark skin, close-cut jet black wavy hair, and broad shoulders. Even in his sorrow, he was an extremely attractive man. I brushed lint off of my husband's jacket, took him by the hand, and walked with him to the car.

The sun peaked out from behind the heavens, as we made it to the church. The processional of family and friends seemed miles long behind Jalen and I while the distinctive scent of the flowers increased the aura of grief. A smooth melodic arrangement of *Amazing Grace* floated through the air and Jalen squeezed my hand as sorrow rushed over him. Looking up at Jalen's face, I gave him a reassuring nod as we made it closer to the front of the church. In response to my support, Jalen held his head up and pushed his shoulders back taking each step slowly. The pink coffin was open and sat directly ahead of us. Once we were at Mama's side—Jalen let my hand go and affectionately touched his mother's face for the last time. He bent over, kissed her on her forehead and whispered, "I love you Mama. Thank you for everything. Now rest."

Watching my husband bravely say good-bye to his mother caused me to lose my composure. I began to quake with grief and my knees became weak. Jalen then stood straight up and braced me around my waist. I looked at Mama long and hard. She looked very peaceful and pretty. She died before the cancer was able to ravish her small frame and therefore looked not much different today than she did a year ago. I reached out and touched the flower that she wore on her dress and then ran my fingers over the family portrait of Jalen, Kylen, Kaylen, and me that was in her coffin. "Bye mama." The words left my mouth in a whisper. I then turned to face Jalen, and signaled that I was ready to sit down. He wiped the tears from my eyes and we made our way to our seats hand in hand.

The front pew was only feet away from Mama's coffin. The walk to our seats seemed long partially because my feet did not seem to react to the orders that my mind was giving. I stood about three feet from the pew frozen in pain and disbelief. Jalen gently tugged at my arm, urging me to continue the short walk to our seats. However, I was overcome by the moment, exhausted from the occasion, and most of all devastated by what I saw next. Several feet behind me in the processional of family and friends stood Alex, dressed in black, with tears running down her face uncontrollably. She was being consoled and almost held up by two of Jalen's cousins. I stared in utter shock at the display of emotion that she was putting on. Why was she in this line? Why was she being consoled as if she had lost a loved one? Why did Jalen not seem surprised by her presence? As I stood in place, the line stopped moving. It was as if everyone in the church was waiting to see how I was going to respond to this awkward situation. I decided at that moment that I would not disrespect my mother-in-law's funeral by doing the one thing that my mind was telling me to do.

I gently removed my arm from Jalen's grasp and continued to my seat with my head up and no emotion on my face. As we sat, I slid my bottom a little to the left and put a few inches of space between Jalen and me. Noticing my signs of anger, Jalen put his left hand on my knee and whispered in my ear, "Mel, don't do this here. We will talk about this later." The organist began to play *I Give it Back to Thee* as the processional began to move again. This was always one of my favorite songs so I ignored Jalen and put what little energy I had left into celebrating Mama's life.

Alex approached the coffin slowly, pretending to become weak once she was directly in front of the casket. Sean, Jalen's cousin, grabbed Alex at her elbow and helped her to her seat. When she passed Jalen and me, Alex stopped for a second and looked at Jalen and then continued to her seat crying even more controllably. It was a disgraceful showing and Jalen dropped his head in shame. I looked over my shoulder at Kaiya who was sitting in the back corner of the church with Victoria and Kylen. When her eyes met mine, Kaiya held up Mama's obituary and mouthed, "look at this!" There was excitement and anger in her eyes as she did this. Jalen and his aunt had taken care of the obituary. Therefore, I was unaware of what could have caused her to want me to read it right now at this very moment. I looked at Kaiya and nodded my head, but then began to fan myself with the obituary. The line continued to move and it looked as if about 200 people were still left to view Mama's body for the final time.

I opened the obituary and began to read it. As I read the first line, Jalen reached out and grabbed the obituary out of my hand. The haste with which he moved startled me and thus caused me to jump a little. Eyebrows raised, I looked over at Jalen as if he'd lost his mind. Realizing where we were, I politely grabbed the obituary back from Jalen's very tight grip and continued reading. "Mel," Jalen whispered very loudly this time. "I said, not now!"

"What do you mean by not now? Jalen, I am just looking at the obituary." I managed to control my anger and picked up my reading on the second line of the obituary. It was very well written and included a very beautiful poem to Mama. As I made it down to her surviving loved ones; I reached my breaking point. There in black and white it read,

> "Pearl is survived by one son Dr. Jalen Starks (Melany). She also leaves 4 grandchildren: Kylen Starks, Kaylen Starks, Chase Sanders, and Chris Sanders."

The program hit the ground with the force of a boulder as once cloudy details began to fill my mind in a vivid fashion. I remembered Kylen at the pediatrician and how he seemed to know Alex's child. I remembered how Kylen always had a little boy with him at Mama's house when he went to visit. That was when he began to say the word "Tase". I then realized why I couldn't ride with Jalen to drop Kylen off. Tears ran down my face uncontrollably as I remembered the last, most devastating detail. "Mel, we have more in common than you think." I remembered Alex saying this vividly. I began to shake as I pictured those words leaving Alex's lips.

Jalen touched my arm in an effort to get my attention. "Don't touch me! You are a liar and I am through, Jalen. Through!"

"Mel, please don't do this here. Not at my mama's funeral. Please, let's just talk about this when we get home."

"Home? Whose home? Jalen, we don't have a home anymore. And I could care less about this being her funeral. She lied to me too. So as far as I am concerned—all of ya'll can go straight to…" I was unable to finish my sentence. My respect for the building would not allow me to. I stood up in front of the entire church and his low down family and walked to the corner where Kaiya sat with my kids. As I walked, every one stared and whispered. I could actually hear several of the comments. One of Jalen's younger cousins leaned over and whispered to a friend of the family, "I guess she finally read the obituary." Another person said, "Bout time she found out. They have been lying to that poor girl for years."

As the comments flew across the room and the whisper turned into quiet chatter—I marched up to Ky and grabbed Victoria from her arms. "Let's go baby. Ky, get Kylen and let's go."

"I'm right behind you." As we made our way out of the church, I looked at Alex's face. Her expression was not the same troublesome expression that she usually wore. Rather it was sorrowful this time, as if she too felt pain. I could not look her in her eyes though. I was too embarrassed, angry, and hurt; looking at her would give what little power I had away. Not only did this funeral represent Pearl's death; it represented the death of the last four years of my life. With my only real family with me—I walked out of the church and out of my hellish marriage.

Chapter 8

The days after learning of Jalen's secret family were bitter-sweet. I felt cheated and betrayed by Jalen's entire family. It was as if everyone helped to create this fairy tale portrait of Jalen for me, all knowing that I was married to a lie. There were so many times that his family referred to Kylen as the first born grandson. For every time that I thought about this I began to feel nauseated.

The day that I left the funeral Jalen and his family called me hundreds of times. After storming out of the church, I went home, immediately packed our bags, and left. Kaiya owned a condo that Jalen was unfamiliar with and she was perfectly fine with the kids and me staying there indefinitely. As I suspected, Jalen harassed Kaiya in an attempt to learn of my whereabouts, however she stood strong and after about two weeks of being rejected, he gave up and decided to accept the awful fate of our marriage. I did not want to see Jalen nor did I want to talk to him or his scandalous cousins and aunts. I only wanted to be left alone to learn how to deal with my life as a single mother and career woman.

It would be a lie to say that I didn't hurt or that I didn't cry every night over the loss of my husband and the only family that I had known for years. Truly, I grieved for days and nights on end, and every morning I prayed for the pain to end or for God to give me the strength to bear it.

I had been without Jalen for about five weeks and the time had come for me to begin to face the world again. I woke up with a nervousness that tugged at my stomach and made me want to cover my head with the blankets and not come out for days. However, this morning, I managed to throw the covers back and prepare to take the world head on and with no regrets.

I stood in my closet looking at the rows of clothing and scratched my head. In my depression, I had been neglecting my hair and it felt crunchy to the touch. After standing there for about ten minutes, I decided on a cute jogging suit and a pair of AirMax. It was cute yet effortless, I grinned to myself as I held it up in front of the mirror.

Remembering, the issues that I was having with my hair, I picked up the phone and called Kaiya. I laughed to myself as I thought about the sarcastic comments that would leave her mouth when she heard my voice. She answered on the second ring.

"Hey Ky!"

"Oh my God." Kaiya exclaimed, "The dead has arisen."

"Whatever. Can I come and get my hair done? Honey, I look a hot mess."

"Yeah can you get here in an hour?"

"Sure Ky. See you in a little bit." I hung up the phone with a smile on my face. Kaiya always had a way of making me smile when things seemed very bleak. I hopped off the bed and danced over to the CD player. Destiny's Child floated through the house as I began to dress myself for the day.

After I was dressed I turned up the music and danced as it followed me into Kylen and Victoria's room. Kylen was lying in his bed watching Elmo, and Victoria was asleep in her crib. I scooped Kylen up off of the bed and spun him around in circles. He giggled and yelled, "Mommy" as he held his head back and his hands in the air. as I played with my son, I realized that I was happy for the first time in almost a year. Though it wasn't the joy that I often desired for myself—it was still a very content acceptance with my current situation that allowed me to feel some moments of happiness.

I shuffled Kylen into the bathroom and placed him in the warm water as we sang our ABC's. Bath time was always his favorite time of the day. I watched as Kylen splashed and fumbled through The Alphabet Song, unable to pronounce any of the letters correctly. The smile on his face and the gleam in his eye was priceless and I realized at that moment that my kids were the thing that kept me holding on.

Kylen covered his eyes as I rinsed the shampoo from his hair. Suddenly, he removed his hands from his eyes and looked up at me with very loving and serious eyes. "Mama, you yook pretty. You smile." Though he had trouble pronouncing the word look, he was more observant and articulate than most toddlers his age. Over the past few weeks, my sadness had affected my ability to be there for my kids and he too realized that Mommy was back. I held Kylen's face in my hands and kissed his forehead, "Kylen, yes I am smiling. You and Kaylen make me smile. Mama loves you very very much."

"Mama?" Somehow I knew what was coming next, but even knowing it did not prepare me to answer it. I looked at Kylen as he finished his sentence. "Where's Daddy?"

"Daddy is at home. You will see him soon okay baby."

"Okay, I miss Daddy." Kylen looked a little sad as he expressed his feelings. "Me too." I replied as I splashed water in his face. "Now get out of this water and give me a hug." I pulled Kylen out of the water and kissed his wet tummy as he laughed and kicked. He dried off quickly and ran to his room bare-bottomed and laughing. I dried up the water that he left on the floor and quickly followed Kylen to his room and dressed him.

I was just about to get Victoria up to have her bath when I heard the doorbell. I put Kylen's favorite DVD in the player and went to answer the door. Reece was supposed to come and watch the kids while I went out today so I went down the steps quickly two at a time, expecting it to be her. It had been months since I'd seen Reece and I was very anxious to see her face.

I grabbed the doorknob and began to turn it. Just then, nervousness arose in my gut. I knew that it would not be Reece on the other side of the door. Slowly, I looked through the peephole. Standing a few inches away, on the opposite side of the door was Jalen. I saw the tops of the flowers that he was holding in his shaky hand. Though I knew that he saw me looking through the peephole, I yelled out, "Who is it?"

"Baby it's me—Jalen." I nervously smoothed my hair and adjusted my top before opening the door. "I'm not your baby. If I am not mistaken you have two of those with Alex." I opened the door and motioned him into the house with obvious frustration. "So Jalen, how did you find out where I lived?"

"I have my ways. But Mel, that's not important. What is important is that you and my kids come home. I miss you so much and my life has been so off track since you left. I hate that you had to find out that way but both Chase and Chris were born before we got married. I should have told you about them but I thought I would lose you and I just couldn't risk it. Yes, I did cheat before we got married but as your husband—I have been completely faithful to you."

"Faithful hell Jalen! You have been with Alex our whole marriage. I did everything to keep you away from her but you chose to keep her in our lives. Every time I looked up, there she was flaunting in my face. You even had Kylen and her child playing together—but you want me to believe that you were faithful to me. I'm sitting at the funeral like a fool and everyone was watching me while I read about your secret kids Jalen. Your kids! Your mama kept it from me, Victor kept it from me, and all of your cousins, aunts, and uncles kept it from me too! As far as I am concerned all of ya'll can go to hell. Now if you don't mind—I need to get my kids dressed. Can you please get the hell out of my house?"

"No Mel." Jalen spoke softly and seemed unsure of what he was saying. "I'm not leaving here without seeing my kids."

"Oh here we go with that. You weren't thinking about your kids when you were gone for days with Alex. You didn't even rush home when Victoria and I were in critical condition in the hospital. But now, you want to see your kids. Yeah right."

"Melany," Jalen had the same tired tears running down his face that had been used and reused for years. They no longer had an effect on me. "You all have been gone for over a month. I miss my babies. Can I please see them? Please." Just as I fixed my lips to repeat no. Kylen came running into the living room smiling and yelling, "Daddy! Daddy!"

"Hey big guy! Oh, I missed you so much." Jalen hugged Kylen tight and kissed his forehead repeatedly as Kylen hugged his father back. As I watched them hug, I began to resent the situation that Jalen had forced our kids into. For my entire life, I longed for a secure and loving family of my own. I wanted a family where the father woke up in the same home as the kids, and where breakfast was served at the table by Mama while Dad read the morning paper. For years I thought that Jalen and I could have that family. Now I was feeling the resentment of knowing that it wasn't going to be possible, at least not with Jalen.

I snapped out of my daydream to an empty room. Kylen was holding his dad's hand and leading him up the stairs to Victoria. My angry heart was telling me not to let him go up the stairs of my home. It felt as if him having access to my home would eventually lead to him having access to my heart. That was one thing I could not allow.

The doorbell rang just as I opened my mouth to stop Jalen from going upstairs. Exasperation overcame me and I opened the door and surrendered to the idea that Jalen would have to have a relationship with our kids. Reece stood before me with an unsure look on her face. She had seen Jalen's car in the driveway and knew right away that this was going to be an awkward situation that she was walking into. I hugged Reece and greeted her, "Hey girl. Come on in."

"Uhh is that Jalen's car outside? Is it a bad time?"

"Yeah it's his car. He is visiting with the kids. I am going to leave before he comes back down here and makes me go off. Whatever you do, don't let him out of your sight with my kids. And they are not—I repeat—are not to leave this house with him." I grabbed my purse and keys off of the table and rushed out of the house. The tension in there was choking the life out of me. As I walked to the car, I inhaled deeply and wrapped my mind around the reality of my new single life.

My hair had new life and bounced while I told Kaiya about Jalen's surprise visit. Neither she nor I had any idea how he found out about my new place. Kaiya was completely supportive of my point of view. She listened intently as I vented to her. Tears welled up in my eyes and dried up at the very next sentence. Throughout my conversation with her, my emotions ranged along a very wide spectrum of happiness and sadness. Finally, when I paused as if I was finished with my sentence, Kaiya placed her hand on my shoulder and spoke. "Mel, you may not want Jalen as your husband, but those kids still deserve him as their father. You know how our rolling stone daddies screwed us up. Please don't create the same life for my Godchildren."

I know Kaiya, I just don't want to surrender part of my life to him and then lose the rest."

"Melany Lanae, now I know you know yourself better than that. Ain't nobody thinking nothing about Jalen. You just need to do what is best for your kids. Girl, you hair is fierce." Kaiya left the subject right there and moved on to her normal silly self. She was laughing and joking with the other patrons in the shop; I was in a serious mood however. I grabbed my purse and quietly left out of the shop. "Bye Kaiya," I spoke quietly with my head down as I pulled the door closed. Tears of confusion ran down my face—I wiped my eyes and mentally devised a plan for the next chapter in my life.

My next stop was the catering business. I hadn't been there to check on things in at least seven weeks, so I needed to go by and make sure that it was still standing and functioning. The faces of the employees lit up when I walked into the kitchen. Between the hugs and pats on the back, they all seemed to have sympathetic looks on their faces and spoke soft kind words. It was obvious that every one knew about what was going on.

I took a few minutes to catch up on personal things with the employees before catching up on the business. The employees told me about Jalen's numerous interrogation sessions that he'd had with them over the past few weeks. He acted totally desperate to find out where I lived. Of course there were the normal, "I knew he was too good to be true" statements, followed by, "he didn't deserve you anyway." While these comments were made with good intentions—they made me feel foolish, gullible, and naïve. Well before I finished up the intended business, I became overwhelmed by the attention that my life was getting. It was as if the walls were closing in on me while the whole world sat by and watched.

I sifted through the account receipts, quickly scanning them and estimating our numbers for the past few weeks. I turned the pages by their corners, paying little attention to the patrons and clients names at the top of the sheets. Leah, one of my servers, sat in a chair in my office and rambled to me about her new boyfriend. Her words met my ears with insignificance; love didn't live here anymore. The pages flipped quickly in hand, sticking to each other ever so often. When I finally got to the last sheet, the name, Alexandra Sanders, stood out at the very top of the sheet. We had catered a party for her months earlier, right under my nose. I dropped the stack of papers as I fumbled my things and stuffed them into my briefcase. Without saying good-bye to anyone, I hustled out of the door mission-focused.

Alex's address was on the invoice. I wanted to pay her a visit. I needed to show her just how much damage that she caused my life. I needed to go to her house and destroy her home, just as she did mine. The more the vengeance grew inside of me, the harder I bit down on my lip; I tasted bloody revenge. My mind was set and I was on my way to see Jalen's little girlfriend. For once, she would be the hunted and I would flaunt.

Thirty minutes later, I pulled into my driveway and walked up to the house with a feeling of defeat. Even though I had every intention of going to see Alex—my class wouldn't let me stoop that low. Again, I shied away like a puppy with my tail between my legs. It felt as if she now owned every part of me: my pride, husband, thoughts, and even my courage. I struggled with the lock as I thought of the two things that she would never have, Kylen and Kaylen Victoria.

Kylen met me at the door soon as I walked in. He was covered in peanut butter and looked absolutely adorable. He hugged me long and tight and when he finally walked away, my shirt was adorned with little peanut butter handprints. I made my way into the den where Reece was rocking Kaylen to sleep. I touched her face, careful not to wake her and then moved to the sofa for some much needed rest. Just after my butt touched the cushion cushion of the couch, the doorbell rang.

"That's probably Jalen, Mel." Reece spoke with her eyebrows raised. "He's called here four times since you left."

"I don't know what he's callin' me for. I am not trying to hear anything he has to say. Could you get that and tell him that I am not here." I laid back and put my feet up on the couch as Reece went to answer the door. Within minutes she came back into the room with a very surprised look on her face. "Melany, you have someone waiting for you at the door."

"What do you mean? No one knows where I stay. Who is it now?"

"I think..." Reece dropped her head as she spoke. "It's Alex."

"Don't play with me Reece!"

"Mel, I am serious. I didn't let her in—but she is still out there." Before Reece could finish her sentence, I was heading up the stairs to change my shoes. I put on some older Nikes, pulled my hair back into a ponytail, removed my earrings and jewelry and headed to the door where my archenemy stood waiting. "Reece, take the kids upstairs and make sure Kylen doesn't come outside." I yelled to Reece as I was throwing the door wide open. Alex stood there and immediately anger flew from my mouth. "Now I know you done lost your mind. You got three seconds to get the hell off of my doorstep. One, two..."

"Wait Mel, I only want to talk to you"

"Three!" Before I knew it, my hand flew across Alex's cheek. While the lick was not too damaging, it was definitely vicious and disrespectful. Alex's face turned sharply with the force and remained turned for seconds after the lick. I braced myself for her retaliation but was instead met with tears. She stood perfectly still crying heavily and sorrowfully and made no attempts to hit me back. Her tears ran quickly and I paused at her weakness. "Oh so now you want to cry. Ain't that some…"

"Melany, I only came here to apologize to you. I didn't mean for things to turn out this way. It really isn't what it looks like."

"What do you mean? Things ain't what they look like? You got two kids by my husband—two whole kids, Alex! You have followed me around and crept around with my husband since I married him. Hell, you even showed up at my wedding—in white. You wanted him that bad—well guess what. Now you got him. Get off my doorstep." I turned to walk back into my house. Within about two steps Alex yelled out, "Mel, I am only seventeen. I loved Jalen because I didn't know any better."

My feet froze mid-step. Slowly, I turned and faced her. There she stood with childlike eyes, in womanly clothes. Her eyeliner was streaking from the tears and her nose was running profusely. I eyed her from head to toe and instantly began to see her for what she was—a child. "How can you be only seventeen when you have a four year old with Jalen? That would make you thirteen when you had Chris."

"Mel, I got pregnant when I was 12. My mama took me to see Dr. Starks when I was about eleven. And…" she paused, never looking up from her feet. "He told me I was pretty. He told me that I was the finest thing he'd ever seen and that I was more mature than any grown woman that he knew. Mel, he only touched me at first. I'd never had anyone to show me any attention so I liked it, I guess. I made excuses to go to the doctor after that and because my Mama worked so much, I had to go by myself.

When I was 12, Jalen gave me a ride home from school. But we didn't go home—we went to his house. We watched movies, ate popcorn and wrestled around like we had been friends forever. The next day he picked me up again and this time he kissed me and asked me if

I wanted to be his little lady. Mel, I was pregnant two months later. I thought he loved me; he said we would be together. He told me If I cared about him enough to keep our secret, that he would always love me and take care of me. We were supposed to get married as soon as I turned eighteen. I believed him and moved out of my Mama's house. He got me a nice place to live and bought me cars, clothes, and jewelry. We were perfect until he met you. That's why I followed you; I was mad and jealous. Mel, Jalen has always taken good care of our kids, but I just couldn't accept him not loving me anymore. I wanted you to leave him, because I knew he would never leave you. I wanted you to find out about me, so I invaded your life every chance I got. I gave up a lot to be with Jalen and have his kids. He took my whole life and I just couldn't let it go."

"Jalen? Are you talking about my Jalen?" I said his name again hoping that she would realize that she had the wrong guy. "Jalen would not do any of that mess. My husband is not a pedophile. Baby girl, you must be mistaken." As I talked, I began to panic. I had two kids with Jalen, one was a girl. How could he be capable of sleeping with a child? I looked into Alex's eyes and saw her pain. While I did go through a lot with Jalen, this poor child had seen worse. Assuming I still didn't believe her, Alex pulled out her driver's license and held them up. Tears welled up in my eyes and I looked long and hard at her date of birth, she was only a child. "Would you please leave my house, Alex? I can't handle this right now—please just go."

"Okay, but here is my number. Call me if you have any questions. I would really like for our kids to know each other—they are brothers and sisters." I barely heard the tail end of Alex's statements. The door closed softly in her face and I stood with my back resting on it, my eyes looking up at the ceiling.

Reece entered the room where I stood and pulled me into a hug. My knees could no longer stand the weight and they soon buckled under the pressure. There I lied in the floor, a crumpled mess with Reece's arms wrapped around me. Never had I met such lows and painful feelings of shame, betrayal and hurt. I was married to a man that I didn't even know and lived a life with him in complete ignorance of the pain that he was capable of causing.

I thought back to Jalen's eyes as he said, "I do." There was nothing in them that told the true story of who he was. When he touched me, it wasn't sickening. His scent was captivating, not the foul odor that one imagines in a child molester. How could he be the one thing that he always proclaimed to hate with a passion?

This time, I didn't try to hold the tears back. I welcomed them into the room. They were my release and my only way of coping at that moment. I wept in Reece's arms, hating everything that my life had evolved into. As Reece comforted me, I realized that she too was relatively young. I paused and looked at Reece in her eyes, "Did Jalen every try anything with you Reece?" I was unable to finish the question without an emotional outburst. "I am so sorry that we have put you in this situation. But Reece, I need you to be honest with me. Did he?"

"No. Mel, Dr. Starks has been nothing but decent and kind to me. So don't you worry about me. You just relax and take your time. I will stay with the kids tonight."

Though I felt relief that Jalen had behaved himself with the sitter, it didn't comfort the sick feeling that I had. My entire life and existence was now in question. Slowly, I stood to my feet, testing them first to make sure that they could hold my weight. I grabbed my keys from my purse and ran to the car.

The drive to Jalen's house was long and quiet. The silence continuously rang in my ears. I allowed the tears to run down my face uninterrupted—I was too weary to dry them. *Not gone Cry,* by Mary J. played on the radio and it only intensified the sadness that I felt. I pulled over to the side of the road and put my head on the steering wheel. The silent tears evolved into violent sobs. When nothing was left, and I had cried all I had, I continued to Jalen's house.

I approached the circle drive slowly and took a deep breath before I got out of the car. As I stood by my car, I looked at the house; darkness surrounded it as the sun descended for the evening. I rang the doorbell once and waited for Jalen to answer. Impatiently, I rang it again tapping my feet as I waited. Jalen answered the door with a very pleasantly surprised expression on his face. "Hey baby. I'm glad you came by. I knew you would come around."

"Come around. Yeah Jalen, I have come around alright." As I spoke, I slapped Jalen across his face with all of the strength I could muster. Shock controlled his body and he stood absolutely still hoping that I would go away. "I talked to Alex today." I held my index pointed at his face as I spoke. "You are a sick bastard!"

"Mel, you can't listen to anything that she tells you."

"Jalen, how old is Alex?" I reached out and mugged his face, continuing the interrogation, "I said—how old is Alex? While you are standing there looking stupid, you need to be answering my question. You know what? Don't even waste your breathe answering. You and I both know that she is seventeen. Were you that desperate? Did you need to sleep with a twelve year old girl and make babies with her too? You took that girl's innocence and her virginity. You made me think that she was just some crazy woman following us around, when all the time she was a victim of yours. You knew you were raping a child.

Jalen you are a sick, sick man. And your mama—please don't even get me started on her. She was just as wrong as you were. She knew the whole time that you were sleeping with a child and she hid your secret too. And, you had the nerve to accept a Man of the Year award. I promise you this—you will pay for all of this. One way or the other, Jalen you are going to pay."

"Mel. Wait baby, it's not like that. I didn't rape anybody. She wanted it. She seduced me like a grown woman. Man, she is a little lying slut—she is only mad because I married you. I never loved her, Mel. I love you. Please don't do this." Jalen was on his knees hugging my legs as he begged for forgiveness. "Please baby. I need you and my family."

"Need me? No what you need is help. You make me sick. I can honestly say that I hate you now Jalen. I wish I never met you." As I spoke to Jalen, my voice remained calm, soft, yet enraged. Jalen sat on his knees looking up at me with an expression of absolute surprise. He never imagined that I could be this person that stood before him. In all of the years that he dogged me—he never met this side of Melany Starks. "Like I said Jalen, you are going to pay." I pulled my leg away from his grasp and walked back to my car. Full of rage, I popped my trunk and pulled my ten pound dumbbell from the trunk. I took slow and deliberate steps towards Jalen's Mercedes, armed and contemplating my next move. Standing about a foot away from his precious baby, I threw the dumbbell through the windshield. Turning to face Jalen, I smiled evilly at him, "You and I are done Dr. Starks. Oh, and baby boy, you are going to get yours—trust." One could very easily say that I lost my mind that day. But who knew that I would soon lose much more.

Chapter 9

▼

Only days after learning the truth about Jalen, I filed for a divorce. Sheila, my attorney, was a cut-throat bitter divorce' and the proceedings had already began to show the signs of being very tumultuous. I married Jalen at a very young and naïve age, and therefore knew very little about protecting my assets. Back then I never considered the fact that Jalen and I would ever divorce.

The day after Jalen proposed, I was in a dream world. He brought a prenuptial agreement to me and handed it to me only moments after telling me how much he loved me and how he would cherish me forever. Believing this, I never read the agreement or thought for one second to question what I was agreeing to. I would have signed anything to have Jalen.

Now, weeks into our divorce, I found out the terms that I agreed to four years ago. I had signed away my life and my mother's legacy. According to the terms of the agreement, in the event of divorce prior to ten years of marriage I would leave the marriage with the same dollar amount that I entered it with. The worse part was this; the party with the greater income would retain rights and ownership to all businesses and real property between the two of us. Of course Jalen had more money than I had. He was a doctor with a very popular thriving practice and I was a semi-successful caterer. However, because I allowed Jalen to become a partner in the catering business, it too was considered community property within this divorce. Under the terms of the prenup that I signed, I was going to lose my mother's catering business to Jalen.

When Sheila informed me of this, I was crushed. I felt like a complete failure. My mother had cherished her business and she left it to me. How could I let this happen. Sheila and I were very determined to hold on to "A Touch of Class." She fought hard on my behalf and I found myself in constant prayer for the first time in my life.

In order to expedite the process, we decided to schedule a mediation hearing in which the decision of the mediator would be final and binding. Sheila and I accepted this with optimism, hoping that the influence that Jalen and Victor had within the community would not result in bias from a private mediator who wasn't an elected official.

The day of the mediation, I met with Sheila for lunch to discuss the last few important details of my case. We would present all of the dirt that I had on Jalen and would not spare his reputation at all. He had to be seen for the man that he was and Sheila would see to it that he was.

As we made the walk from the parking lot into the office of the mediator, Sheila and I passed Jalen and Victor walking. Jalen looked down at his feet when we passed him and was careful not to make eye contact with me. Victor eyed me viciously and nodded his head coldly as he greeted us, "Ladies, good afternoon." He had a smug look on his face and was no longer the friendly brotherly person that I trusted for so many years. Sheila returned the icy professionalism and replied, "Afternoon, Counselor Laines."

We entered into the conference room and sat directly across from each other. Neither Jalen nor I looked at one another but Sheila and Victor eyed each other competitively. The mediator, Terri Sloane, came in sat and began the proceedings. She looked stern as she spoke, "First I would like to remind both parties that the agreements made here and today are final and binding. I would first like to hear from the Petitioner, Mrs. Starks."

As Sheila presented my case, I began to gain confidence in my ability to walk out of this marriage with the three things that were important to me, Kylen, Kaylen Victoria, and A touch of Class. The business represented my past and my kids represented my future and I considered them to be necessities in my life. She told of Jalen's infidelity, of his involvement with a minor, and of the kids that he did not disclose. Sheila told about me having the baby without Jalen and that he was out of town at a convention that never happened. Most of all she pointed out the fact that I was tricked into signing an agreement that was grossly unfair and would cause me to lose my mother's legacy. As she spoke, my lip quivered and my eyelids fought to hold back the tears. After making a strong case and visibly moving the mediator, Sheila rested our case.

Listening to details of my life drained me, so the mediator allowed us to take a short break in order for me to gain my composure. After the break, Victor began to present his case. He presented me to the mediator as a gold-digger who only wanted Jalen for his money. He denied Jalen's relationship with a seventeen year old Alex, however admitted to small acts of infidelity. He even called me incompetent to run a business or a household, citing the fact that I had a caretaker for the kids even on days that I wasn't working, as well as my days of depression when I failed to check on the books at our catering business. While his mudslinging was limited, he closed with the fact that while the agreement may appear to harsh it was necessary that he retain ownership of both businesses to ensure that our kids would be well-taken care of and secure in the future.

After taking a moment to sort out her papers, Terri began to speak, "It was an awful injustice committed far before the marriage began. The prenuptial agreement is extremely one-sided. Mrs. Starks was lied to and cheated on throughout this marriage and its end should be placed solely on the shoulders of Dr. Starks. While my sentiments go out to you Mrs. Starks, I have to rule within the allowance of the law. The prenuptial agreement is a contract between two parties, one which both parties signed and agreed to. It is very important to research and read it carefully before signing said agreement. Because it wasn't signed under duress or perjure, and both parties were in a sound mental state it is binding. We will however need to settle on the custody of the children."

"She can keep them." Jalen blurted it out quickly and carelessly. "I just wanna be able to see 'em when I get ready to."

"Dr. Starks, just a moment ago, your counsel stated that you wanted to own the businesses for the welfare of your kids, however now when discussing custodial rights—you quickly decide that you don't want them. I find that a bit interesting. However as you wish, full custody of both children shall be awarded to Mrs. Starks. I will however, adjust the divorce decree to include spousal and child support payments totaling $15,000.00 per month. This will include $10,000 for child support and the remaining $5000 for spousal support. If there is nothing further—all parties may be excused."

I sat completely still as Victor and Jalen hugged and walked out of the room bubbling with ego. Sheila sat beside me and stared at me in sympathy before speaking, "Well, at least you got something. The mediator understood your case and knew that Jalen was wrong. She couldn't break your contract but at least she made him pay more than usual. I'm so sorry, Melany. I did the best that I could, but that agreement was solid and you signed it. After a few months we can seek an increase in your payments and before long he will be paying you all of the profits from your mother's business."

"Sheila, it's not about the money. It is about having a part of my Mama. Now I don't have it or her." Slowly, I rose to my feet and gathered my things. Dragging one foot in front of the other, I made my way to the parking lot without looking behind me. I had nothing to look back at and nothing to look forward to.

Losing everything in my divorce to Jalen felt like losing my mother all over again. I fell deep into depression and became less than a mother to Kylen and Kaylen. I never left the house unless absolutely necessary and even then would try first to find someone else to take care of necessities for me. Kaiya stood by for weeks and allowed me to wallow in my self-pity, finally when she had watched me self-destruct for long enough; she stepped in and began the long process of helping me to rebuild my life.

Slowly, I began to come to grips with my new life. I started by getting my kids dressed and fed in the mornings and taking them for walks. We had picnics, played at the park, and enjoyed each other every day. Kaiya and I began to look around at commercial properties. Together we came up with the idea to open a new catering business and name it in my mother's honor. It would be called, "A Real Touch of Class." It would be a recognized name, made better. I was sure that it could be a success, because I made the first one a success.

I was on my way to meet up with Kaiya. It was a warm sunny day and I was all smiles. I had located the most perfect little space for my new company. I snapped pictures of it, got the information for it and was on my way to share it with Kaiya. She and I planned to invest equally in it. In between the payments that Jalen was making and the money that I left the divorce with, I had plenty of money to work with. Things were beginning to look up and I started to feel like Melany again.

I nodded my head to the music as I made my way through the traffic. It was extremely heavy today, which was unusual for this time of the day. I glanced in my rear view mirror to see Kylen sitting in the back seat dancing with the music too. Realizing that I was looking at him, a smile spread across his face and he began to simulate dancing even harder. He would move his upper body from left to right, keeping his arms bent and close to his body. I turned the music up loudly and began to dance with my son. "I'm every woman, it's all in me." I sang with the music. The words gave me encouragement in the moment and I celebrated my new freedom and ambition in the car with my son. The traffic was now creeping along at a slow pace. Within minutes, the reason for the jam came in to view. It was an accident directly ahead and in the far left lane. I became relieved at the sight, only because I was ready to get past it and hurry to my destination.

As I passed the accident I realized that the car and its passengers were very familiar. There stood Alex outside of her car bleeding visibly from her forehead. In the backseat of her car were Chris and Chase. Part of me wanted to continue past them as if I didn't know them, but without thinking I began to veer to the left. After putting my car in park in the left hand shoulder of the expressway, I got out of the car and walked towards Alex. She was crying uncontrollably and shaking. When she saw me coming, her tears slowed for a second before continuing at a greater rate. "Alex." I touched her on her back as I spoke. "Are you okay? Do you need any help?"

"I called the police on my cell phone, they are on the way. Some jerk hit from behind really hard and sped off. I hit my head on the steering wheel, but I am okay. The boys are okay too, they are just a little shaken up. Thanks for stopping."

"No problem. Kylen is in the backseat of my car. I am going to go wait in my car with him; I will come back and check on you again in a few minutes." I walked to my car and sat down, deep in thought. Was I out of my mind? No one in their right mind would stop and help the woman who had been sleeping with her husband. So why was I sitting here? As I asked myself questions, my mind continued answering them. She isn't a woman—she's a child who was forced to play the role of a woman by a sick man. She would never be in this situation if Jalen had not taken advantage of her at the age of twelve. Her mother gave up on her and she was all alone to deal with grown-up issues. While she did make some huge mistakes, I completely understood and sympathized with her position.

My thoughts were interrupted by the sirens of the police and an ambulance. I glanced behind me and realized that the ambulance was coming for Alex. The blood was running from her head wound profusely. Chris and Chase became more upset by the second. I got Kylen out the car and placed him on my hip as I walked back to Alex's car. She was now sitting on the hood of her car with her head down in noticeable pain and unable to look up at me. The EMT began to look at Alex as the policeman surveyed the car's damage. Because it was a hit and run, the question was not of liability, only of the identity of the missing driver.

Alex was unable to clearly answer the questions of the policeman and stared at him dazed as he spoke to her. There was an EMT on her right and a policeman on her left. The EMT then concluded that Alex needed to be taken to the emergency room because she was clearly suffering from a concussion. She also needed to have the cut stitched up. I decided at that moment that I would help her. Forgiveness for her was placed in my heart and I stepped into action. "Alex…Alex?" I spoke slowly and loudly so that she would here me through the fog that was clouding her mind. She turned very slowly and looked at me, "Mel?"

"Alex, I am going to take Chris and Chase with me. They are really scared right now, plus Kylen would love to hang out with them anyway. I am going to put my phone number in your pocket and whenever you get to feeling better you can call me. I will bring them home to you when you're ready."

"Mel thanks but, I can't ask you to do that. Are you sure it will be okay? I don't want to inconvenience you."

"It's no problem. You just take care of yourself."

"Melany…" Alex paused and stared at me long and hard. Though no words were spoken we clearly understood each other for the first time. "Thank you so much."

"Okay, take care." Slowly I walked Kylen back to the car. I adjusted his car seat to make room for his brothers. As I piled each child into the car, I looked closely at them and realized that they both closely resembled Kylen. They both had really dark curly hair, long eyelashes, and dark complexions. Their faces were stained with tears and clouded with doubt. The similarities between Kylen and his brothers were uncanny. Kylen and Chase lit up when they saw each other; they were not only brothers-they were pals. I listened to their giggles the entire way home, moved by their happiness.

Once home, I ordered pizza for the boys and played with Kaylen. Kaiya came over to visit and to meet the kids. While she said that she was coming to check on me—I knew that she was only coming because Alex's kids were there. She keyed into the house without even knocking, "Hey, where is my handsome little man?" She yelled for Kylen. Within in seconds, Kylen came running around the corner and right into Ky's arms. In close pursuit were Chris and Chase. Kaiya's eyes grew big when she saw the boys. With her hands over Kylen's ears, Kaiya whispered, "Girl they look just like Jalen's low-down self. Honey he know he be makin' some pretty babies." She redirected her attention back to the trio that stood in front of her and began to speak to them. "Well hello. You are some of the cutest little boys. What are your names?"

"I'm Chris." The oldest served as the spokesperson for the duo. "And he is Chase."

"Well hello Chris and Chase. I'm Kaiya. It's nice to meet you." Kaiya grabbed Kylen and began to tickle him and said, "and I already know this handsome little devil." She let Kylen go and he quickly ran away and up the steps with his brothers. His was the youngest so he was always at the back of the pack, but he didn't care. Kylen was completely carefree with his siblings.

Alex called later that evening. She had caught a cab home and was calling to let me know that I could bring the boys whenever it was convenient for me. I agreed to take them home early the next morning. That way she could at least get a good night of medicated sleep. When I hung up the phone with Alex, my mind shifted to Jalen while I shifted into a comfortable position in bed. He hadn't called or checked on the kids since before our divorce. It seemed like he wasn't even concerned at all with the kids; his only concern was taking my mother's business away to hurt me. Now that he had what he wanted, the kids were pushed to the bottom of his priority list. It seemed that Alex didn't matter to him, anymore either. I wondered why she had to take a cab home from the hospital. Where was Jalen now? He cared enough for her when we were married to leave me to deliver our child by myself. Where did all of that passion for Alex go now that he was single?

I arrived at Alex's condo at around eleven the next morning. I felt mixed emotions of anger, embarrassment, and closure as I realized that I had seen this address on many of the bills that came through the house during my marriage. Jalen had completely paid for Alex's home and signed the deed over to her. Maybe it was payment for her silence over the past years. I knocked on the door and a smiling Alex answered in Spongebob pajamas. Grinning to myself, I was in awe of just how juvenile her attire was. Jalen was really tripping when he chose to involve himself with her.

When Alex saw her boys, she lit up and picked them up one in each arm. She opened the door widely and motioned for us to come in. Kylen ran in and followed the boys to their room while I followed Alex into her living room with Kaylen in my arms. The room was furnished with nice leather furniture and had walls that were bare for the most part. She had pictures of her sons on the coffee table and on the entertainment center. She had one picture of Jalen holding the boys on one end table, and on the other one many pictures of herself partying at the club. The room itself spoke of her immaturity, causing me to sit with Kaylen in my lap on the edge of my seat in anticipation of my exit from this uncomfortable situation.

Alex came into the living room and sat directly across from me on the couch. She held a coffee mug in both hands and sat with her legs slightly apart. She took one sip, slurping loudly and began to speak thoughtfully, "Mel, I know we met on bad terms, but I really wanna' thank you for looking after my boys yesterday. I really don't have anyone to help me with them, you know since Jalen has stopped helping. My mom is still hot about this whole situation so I don't really talk to her."

"What do you mean Jalen has stopped helping you?" She caught my attention with that statement. "When did he stop?"

"Well Jalen checked out emotionally when he married you. He still sent me money and took care of us financially though; I guess it was so that I wouldn't tell anyone the truth about us. But when I came and told you about me and him—he stopped helping me at all. I figure he'll come around and eventually start back supporting his kids, or I will have to try to get child support."

"Do you work Alex? How are you supporting yourself now?"

"I work part-time doing customer service. This is the first job I have ever had in my life. Working ain't for me. I gotta find me a rich husband, like you did." I was appalled at Alex's nerve. She really did not realize that I was a working successful woman before Jalen. She had the wrong idea about me and about life. I replied to her ignorance in an even tone, "Alex, I owned my own business before Jalen ever came along. You shouldn't wait on a man to come along and take care of you. As you can see now, if someone gives you everything you can be left with nothing if and when they decide to take it away. You have to get your own."

"Yeah right." Alex twisted her hair with her index finger as she spoke. There was a very uncomfortable pause in the conversation and I took it as my cue to leave. I knew that she was not in a place at that moment to recognize the need for maturity. She only recognized her need to make ends meet—by whatever means necessary.

"Well Alex", I stood to my feet as I spoke. "We are going to go now. I have a million things to take care of today and I have to meet the sitter at my house. I really hope you feel better. You take care." By the time I finished the sentence, I was standing in her doorway waiting for Kylen. Once Kylen was there with me, I walked out of her house turning one time to say good-bye. Alex looked at me thoughtfully and replied, "Melany, thanks again. Bye and bye to you too sweet girl. Ooh Mel, she is getting so big. I'll see ya'll." She touched Kaylen's hands as we walked away.

As I made my way to the car, I thought about Alex's life and began to appreciate mine a little more. Silently, I thanked my mother for everything that she had done to make sure that I would be okay after she was gone. Even in death, I had more support from my mother than Alex had from hers alive. That support had made all of the difference in my life.

It had been about two weeks since my visit to Alex's strange world and I still thought of her everyday. My heart wanted very badly to reach out to her. She had seen so much at such a young age that her actual perception of life and love had been tragically distorted. I was unable to ignore the fact that she would have had a better chance at being a responsible semi-productive young lady, if Jalen hadn't stolen the most crucial years of her life. Though I had several thoughts of her, I managed to occupy my time with my kids and my business plans.

The kids had a doctor's appointment this morning. Victoria had a terrible ear infection and Kylen seemed to be catching a little something as well. After signing my kids in at the doctor, I began to write out the check for a co-payment. The nurse then looked up at me with an awkward expression and said, "I'm so sorry Ms. Starks, we will need payment on the balance that you have as well as payment for today's services upfront. Your insurance has been cancelled and they declined your claims. We called the number that we have on file to inform you but Dr. Starks answered and said that he wasn't responsible for this and that you would have to take care of it on your own. I'm really sorry."

"On my own…he said that he wasn't responsible for his kids' doctor bills and I have to take care of it on my own." I stood in front of the desk in utter disbelief. I could not believe that my husband was now abandoning his own children. He knew that I didn't have a job and that we were relying on his insurance. He also knew that Kaylen needed to see the doctor very regularly to monitor her for any delayed health issues that she may have received during my pregnancy.

I looked around and noticed that people were looking. In an effort to save face; I smiled and agreed to pay the balance. "That's no problem, what do I owe you?" I began to write out a new check in the amount of $600.00. As I wrote, I explained the situation to the nurse. "Jalen and I recently divorced and I guess there is some confusion as to who does what. We should have this cleared up in no time. Will this be enough?" I handed her the check and she shook her head saying, "Yes Ma'am I completely understand. This should be more than enough. Would you like me to credit your account for the difference?"

"Yes, that would be fine?" I gathered my things and walked into the waiting room, head held high. As I walked, I dialed Jalen on the cell phone. When I heard his voice answer the phone I began to speak sternly into the phone. "How could you cancel your own kids' insurance? You are a doctor so you know that Kylen and Kaylen need to see the doctor regularly. Do you not care about their health? It's one thing to cancel my insurance—I will be fine. But to do that to your kids—that's just lowdown."

"Melany, I really don't have time for this right now. I got too much to do here at our catering business—or should I say my catering business. You get plenty of child support—pay for it with that." He hung up the phone in my face, leaving a sting of hurt in my heart. There were several things that he said that stood out as hurtful. First of all, he didn't seem to care at all about his kids having insurance. He also taunted me about my mother's business.

I carried on through the appointment as if everything was okay, however I was emotionally regressing. That one phone call to Jalen killed all of the momentum that I had gained over the past weeks. It killed all of the confidence that I gained in my ability to cope with losing my mother years ago and recently losing my marriage too. Other than my two kids and Kaiya, I had no one in this world. All of a sudden, I felt alone—completely alone. There were people in the room with me, I had Kaylen in my lap and Kylen next to me; I still felt alone.

Once the appointment was over, I drove home in complete silence. Kylen got no response to his attempts at playfulness. I didn't respond to Kaylen's whining for attention. I drove the car as if I were dead to the world. My cell phone shook in my hand as I dialed

Reece's number to arrange for her to meet me at my house. I needed to be alone to deal with what I was feeling.

Within moments I was home and drowning in tears and sorrow. One by one, I carried sleeping Kylen and Kaylen into the house and to their beds. After each child was safely tucked in for a nap, I waited outside on the steps for Reece to arrive. As I waited I cried, as I cried, I hurt—finally when the anxiety inside of me began to overflow, Reece pulled into the driveway. She took one look at my face and realized that this time was different from the others. She peered at me with concern as I drove away into the sunset, knowing that if or when I returned, I would be in a different state. Though I had been sad before, this exact moment was not just sadness, my heart was dying.

Chapter 10

The rain came down in a mist, seeming almost weightless. The windows were covered in fog with reminders of the tiny hands of my children. It looked as if God had dipped his brush into black and splattered it on top of darkness. I sat outside of Jalen's unlit parking lot covered in gloom that seemed to swallow me whole. I held my hand up in front of my face and saw nothing. Aside from the tingling sensation that the winter cold brought to my fingertips, there was no feeling within my physical body. I watched the drops of water accumulate in little puddles on the glass until they ran over and down the windshield. Beads of water accumulated in my eyes until they too became too heavy with my burdens and ran down my cheeks. I gripped the gun tightly in my right hand battling the urge to pull the trigger. It felt smooth and cool. At that moment I held redemption, well some twisted form of it I guess.

My hands shook as I waited on something to snap me back into reality and convince me to put the gun down and drive back to my warm home, with my beautiful children. Projections of my life ran through my mind in flashes. Slide after slide, representing crucial moments in my development and self-destruction. Eyes closed, I held my armed hands out and my head began to spin as it did when my absent daddy would swing me in circles as a little girl. I pictured Kylen and Kaylen's first Christmas together. The house smelled of warm cinnamon and pine from the Christmas tree. Suddenly, a cold sweat came over me as the picture switched to their lives without their mother. I buried my mother as a young lady and I managed to screw my life up fully without her. Taking a moment, I began to think about my funeral—what would be said and who would attend? On the front pew, I pictured Jalen's face and wondered if this drastic step would finally pull remorse into his mind.

What had my life represented up until now? Questions flooded my mind, waiting for my heart to provide the summary of my obituary. Could this pain ever be healed? Death seemed so permanent, yet nothing inside of me made me wanted to hold on to life. The suffering was unbearable and my life had lost its value.

The songs on the radio had been solemn that night adding more despair to my current state of mind. The lyrics of *Bohemian Rhapsody* seemed to cry with me and the words were reaffirming my feelings of guilt, hatred, and weariness. "Mama, life has just begun; but now I've gone and thrown it all away. I don't wanna die—but I sometimes wish I'd never been born at all", the velvet smooth voice sang what I too felt in my heart. I agreed with the song and felt it was time to be through with this world—because the world was definitely through with me.

I thought about the events that had pushed me to this point. Laying my head back on the headrest, I allowed my mind to retrace the painful events that led me here. For me, life started on what was truly the most beautiful day of my life. As I sat and relived the past, I began to feel every emotion that I felt as they occurred. I smiled at the good times and cried when I thought of the sad moments. Finally, after I had retraced everything that occurred up to this moment, I snapped back into the present moment completely drained. Like a dose of reality the gloom of the moment reinvented itself.

Again, I picked up the gun and held in my right hand as I traced its grooves with my left index finger. I put it to my head, then dropped my hands in fear. I could not keep a husband, I could not give my kids the attention they needed, and even now—I couldn't even pull the trigger. I had no control over my life and I felt helpless.

I closed my eyes, took a deep breath, and with every intention of going through with it this time—I raised my hand to place the gun to the right side of my temple. Just as it was mid-ways to my head, my phone rang. I paused and looked at it as it glowed in the dark. I knew that I had turned the ringer off; at least I thought I had. Who could be calling now? My cell phone hadn't rang all day, and now it was ringing. I looked at the display and read the caller id. The call was coming from a private number. I made up my mind to ignore it but it continued to ring. I could actually feel an urgent nervous energy run through me with each ring tone.

Normally, the phone would ring only three times before going to voicemail; tonight it rang at least twice that. My hands reacted and picked up the phone. Why did I pick up the phone? Before I answered it, I paused. I mouthed the words hello, but no sound left my mouth.

"Melany? I need to talk to you. I don't have anyone else that I can call. Are you there?"

"Alex?" I whispered into the phone with a shaky voice. "Alex is that you? I can't talk right now. I gotta go."

"Mel, please don't hang up. I know that I haven't been very nice to you, but I don't have anyone else in this world that I can call. Mel, I want something different for my life. I want to be normal. I am a seventeen year old girl with two kids and no high school diploma. I don't want to be this way. Mel can you please listen to me for just a few minutes? You have come through so much and been such an inspiration to me. I thought I had lost everything when Jalen stopped helping me with the kids, but you made me realize that my potential is in me. I have to grow up. It's time to stop depending on other people. I need to be the one that my kids depend on. Are you there???"

"Yeah, Alex I'm here." I listened to Alex ramble while the gun rested in my lap. It no longer felt as if belonged there, I began to fear its power and no longer wanted to be connected with it. "Go on."

"I don't have a mother anymore Melany. I don't have anyone to guide me in the right direction. I believe that God sent you into my life for a reason. I know that I may have made your life very difficult at first and for that I am so sorry. I pray every day that you can find it in your heart to forgive me. I was young, but that does not excuse what happened. I didn't figure out that what was going on with Jalen and I was wrong, until I was about fifteen and I should have stopped it then. By then though, I was in too deep." As Alex spoke she cried heavily and at times lost her ability to vocalize her feelings. She was a child and even in this mature moment of honesty, her words came across in a child-like manner.

I listened to Alex and realized that, though she was a child—she was saving my life. I also began to see some weird humor in what was going on. I laughed to myself as I thought about the fact that I had actually paused from committing suicide to answer the phone. Who would believe that?

At some point during the conversation, the gun ended up in the glove compartment and the rain stopped. It was still dark outside, however it wasn't too dark for me to see the light in my future. God had sent me help in the form of Alex. Purpose began to fill my life within in minutes and my point of view redirected itself.

I always heard that things could change in a blink of an eye, however never felt it to be true until this evening. Only moments ago, I felt that there was only one way out of my misery and that was suicide. Now as I backed out of the parking space and began to drive away from what could have been the biggest and last mistake of my life, I hoped that the worst was behind me.

I drove and listened listened to Alex go on and on about her life. I could tell that everything that she was expressing was a new feeling for her. In her short life, she never had to face the consequences of her actions. She never had a chance to be alone. Now she had to face the true loneliness that her actions with Jalen created. Her mother had abandoned her long before the actual abandonment, in her eyes. How else can you explain a child leaving school everyday with a man and sleeping with him, right under the mother's nose? Alex further explained that she felt the need to place her kids in someone else's care until she was able to provide a more stable home for them. She cried as she said, "Mel, how can a child truly raise a child?"

"Alex, you have already shown that you are capable of taking care of these boys. They love you. Giving them away would be the biggest mistake of your life—believe me, I know." I realized as the words came from my mouth, that I was just about to abandon my kids only moments ago. God spared my life and I felt the need to help Alex with hers.

As Alex and I talked, I drove my car with one destination in mind. Before long I was standing outside—knocking on Alex's door. She answered immediately and fell into my arms. I held her there as she cried tears of anguish. I cried too, but mine were tears of joy.

I spent about three hours with Alex that evening before returning home. When I walked into my house, Reece was sleeping on the sofa, as if she was waiting on me to make it home. I gently rustled her awake, to let her know that I was home and that she could go up and get in the bed. Reece paused and looked at me before saying, "It's so good to see you Mel."

"It's good to see you too Reece. Thank you so much…for everything." Reece reached out and hugged me. As she held me she whispered in my ear, "Joy will come in the morning." I released Reece and stared at her face. She was relatively young yet she held so much wisdom. I nodded solemnly and headed up the stairs. Reece stood and watched, knowing that tonight—I had survived a crisis.

The night drained me physically and I felt relief at the sight of my bed. I kicked off my shoes and plopped down in the bed—still wearing all of my clothes. I laid there waiting on the much needed sleep to overcome my body, yet it didn't come. Something was missing. Never before had I gotten down on my knees and prayed before going to bed. I had always prayed the standard goodnight prayer for Kylen at his bedtime, but never prayed at my own bedtime. Slowly, I slid out of bed and to my knees. My nerves were in knots at the idea of talking to God. Would he would see me as a stranger and not recognize me as his child?

One fear of mine was that the words would not come out intelligently and that he would not be able to understand what my heart truly wanted to tell him. Could I make up for years and years of lost time and communication? How would I make up for years and years of ignoring him? Most of all, how could I ever express my true thankfulness for his intervening on my behalf tonight. I felt as if God had snatched me back from the edge and I had to thank him.

I lowered my head and began to speak to God. My heart pounded as I rushed to vocalize everything that I felt. I became light headed but prayed right through. I thanked him for my beautiful mother, and asked him to rest her precious soul. I thanked him for my health, my strength, my kids, and for his mercy. As I finished thanking him for one thing, praise for three more things would leave my lips. Before long, nearly two hours had passed and I began to feel more like one of God's children. Even after the Amen, I stayed on the floor and cried tears of joy. Within me, I knew that my life would never be the same.

In the weeks that followed, I learned to appreciate my life far more than I ever had before. Every moment that I spent with my kids felt precious. I was renewed permanently—not just until the next crisis came along. I spent time mentoring to Alex and would let her boys stay over at my house while she went out to look for a better job. She enrolled in school the day following our talk and was working on finishing her diploma. If anyone would have looked at my life and compared it to where I had come from—they would say that it was a remarkable change.

Spring had rolled around and I had plans to meet with Kaiya for lunch at our favorite restaurant. The restaurant was small and secluded and quite a ways from the city so we rarely got the chance to go there. I hadn't seen Ky in some time so I was looking forward to spending time with her. I walked into the restaurant excitedly. It had the same 'Old Italian' feel that it had last time Kaiya and I met there.

It was dimly lit with little tea candles at every table. The tiles on the floor were all uniquely shaped cobblestone, and the walls marbled with deep rich tones. As I breathed in the delightful aroma of the kitchen, I noticed Kaiya waving across the room. I rushed towards her, tripping more than once on some of the slightly raised cobblestone tiles on the floor. She stood up from the table and greeted me with a big hug. "Hey stranger. You almost bust your butt running over here." She said as she finger-combed my hair. "Your hair looks good, considering that you haven't been coming to take care of it. But I ain't even gone trip. What's up with you?"

"Girl, I am blessed. Those kids wore me out last night. I am so tired. They miss you Kaiya. We need to go by there when we get through here. If Kylen asks me one more time where you are—I am going to leave him on your doorstep." We sat down at the table and Kaiya looked at me with big happy eyes and said, "Well Mel, you look good. I haven't seen you glow like this in years. I am so happy for you. Oh yeah, guess what. We got approved for the loan, they accepted our offer and we are set to close on the space for "A Real Touch of Class" on the last day of the month. So you need to get them wheels turning because this is going to be your business. I don't want no parts of the decision making—I am only here to support you. I am a silent partner. No, make that a mute partner. Don't ask me my opinion about nothing, zero, zilch—nada!"

"Are you serious? That means we can be open in about two months. I haven't even thought about the décor, the new recipes, marketing or anything. And don't worry about me asking you for any ideas, you have already done more than enough. I am so excited. Kaiya thank you so much for co-signing on the loan. I am all up in your business. Living in your condo, using your credit and oh that reminds me. I need to use your SUV. I am supposed to take Kylen and his brothers out for pizza tonight. I also will need you to stay with Kaylen while I go. Reece is on vacation for the next two weeks."

"You got a lot of nerve telling me what you need." Kaiya was laughing as she spoke. "How do you know I ain't got plans?"

"Girl, you can lay up with Mark anytime. I need you tonight. So is seven okay with you?" As I talked to Kaiya, I notice that her eyes grew wider and wider within seconds. "Mel!" She was whispering excitedly now. "Mel you better turn around and look over in the far corner."

"What are you talking about, girl quit staring." I turned as I spoke. What I saw next, hit me like a kick in the gut. Victor and Jalen were sitting in the darkest corner of the room. They were snuggled romantically at a small table enjoying cocktails. The chemistry between them was not platonic and they peered into each other's eyes in a loving manner. The flicker of the tea candle before them only seemed to heighten the romance between them. I turned back to Kaiya and whispered, "Girl, I must be losing my dang mind. Doesn't it look like they are...?"

"Look Mel." Kaiya grew even more excitedly surprised as she spoke. I turned just in time to see Jalen and Victor share a very passionate kiss. It was as if no one was in the room but the two of them. Kaiya and I watched in total disbelief as the real truth about my life with Jalen unfolded before our eyes. As the kiss ended, Jalen and Victor held hands on the table and continued to stare into each other's eyes; neither of them looked around.

"Kaiya Yvette!" I shockingly shoved Kaiya as I shrieked. "Jalen is gay. He never loved me or Alex. He only used us to make himself look like somebody he wasn't. Alex told me that she never was with Jalen while he was married to me. She said that he wouldn't even speak to her. I assumed that she was lying, but now I know. All of those nights that he was away, Victor was his ride, or his excuse. That's why I could not please him fully. He didn't love me; shoot, he probably didn't even like women-period! He put so much emphasis on thanking Victor at the banquet, and completely overlooked me, his wife. I can't believe this. Girl, I was nothing but a front to him; the perfect front."

"Mel, don't be blaming your self. There is nothing you could have done to prevent this. Jalen is a grown man who makes his own decisions. He is responsible for this nightmare of a marriage that you two had. You are past that now though, you are stronger than you ever were with him. Don't let him drag you back down."

"Drag me down? Girl please, with everything I have been through. Not Jalen or anyone else can drag me down. I am going to go over and say hello, though. You wanna come with me? This is going to be a trip."

Kaiya and I laughed as we got up from the table and approached Jalen and Victor's love corner table. Neither Jalen nor Victor ever saw us coming. "Well hello there Dr. Starks." I replied with a sugary sweet tone. "Hello Counselor Laines." Kaiya spoke with the same sweet tone as well. Both Victor and Jalen looked up at us in shock mixed with shame. Jalen quickly pulled his hand away from Victor's hand and said, "Oh hey Mel, hey Kaiya. When did ya'll get here?"

"We've been here long enough to know the real deal. At least now, I know what really happened, Jalen. Victor you actually fooled me too. I thought we were like family, but I didn't realize we were this close. I mean we were practically sharing a bed. But what can I say; Jalen is a single man now. So you two go right ahead and enjoy each other's company. Oh and Victor dear, tonight while you and Jalen are all cuddled up in bed; if you could, please remind him that he has four children that he needs to check up on. You two lovebirds take care."

I turned and began to walk back to my table briskly, stepping carefully on the shoddy tiles. It would be embarrassing to trip after the grand confrontation that I just had. As I walked I heard the bickering between Jalen and Victor behind me. Victor was angry that Jalen had pulled his hand away from Victor's and accused Jalen of being ashamed of him. Jalen told Victor that he wasn't ready for the world to know and that they wouldn't have been in this situation if Victor hadn't convinced him to come here. Kaiya and I sat at our table, still in amazement. She clapped her hands and said, "Girl, I like the way you handled that. I think Victor is about to cry. But anyway, let them folks do what they want to do. Jalen is a single man—he can date any man he wants to." Laughter erupted from both of us and Jalen hurried out of the restaurant with his head down.

Minutes later, Victor approached our table and offered his apology. "Melany, we didn't mean for you to find out this way. Jalen and I have been in love for years—even before he met you or Alex. I did care for you—I just love Jalen more. I hope you understand."

"Victor, I understand that you and Jalen have ruined my kids' home. I understand that both of ya'll lied to everyone. I also understand that Jalen is a single man now. So you all have the right to do as you please. Don't come over here and expect me to act as if nothing ever happened. It looks to me like Jalen is still frontin'. He ran out of here like a bat out of hell. He doesn't even have time for his kids, but yet and still he is out in public kissing on their so called god-father." I laughed at the irony in that. Victor stood for a moment as he gathered his thoughts and replied. "Jalen and I didn't think that the kids would understand this, that's why he hasn't been around them. Jalen isn't even fully ready to understand this thing between us. We never meant to hurt you, and that is why we were so discreet. Melany, I am really sorry."

"You can save that." Kaiya spoke up. "You can actually raise on up out of our faces ASAP!"

"Yeah Victor, my kids didn't even have insurance anymore. I had to go out and try to get them some immediate coverage somewhere. Jalen took everything from us and you helped him. You really are sorry. At least now you all don't have to fake out of town conventions to play "lovers and friends." You can do what you like—but as far as me ever understanding your position—it's not going to happen. Bye Victor." Kaiya and I stood up and walked past Victor, coldly brushing his shoulder as we strutted out of the restaurant.

Usually these types of incidents would turn into walks of shame for me. This walk was different however. Even knowing that Jalen was involved in a relationship with a man whom I trusted with my family and money, didn't lower my spirits. Kaiya and I made the ride to the Interior Design store without even mentioning Jalen and Victor. She knew that I was in a different place spiritually.

Kaiya and I (well, mostly I) decided on a modern contemporary theme for the catering business. We chose to use deep significant colors and adorn the place with lovely and expensive crystal. My mother always loved crystal and would say "get out the good crystal" when special guests came over. I wanted everyone who came to the restaurant or used our catering services to know that they were special guests.

Finally, things were falling into place for me emotionally. My thoughts were processing information without the extra burden of analyzing every single thing that happened to me. Now, knowing full well what I had overcome, I could step with confidence into what I was about to become.

I arrived at Alex's at about five o'clock to pick the boys up for the weekend. Alex had an exam at school Monday and really needed to study this weekend. She wouldn't have accepted if I offered to baby-sit so I asked her to allow the boys to come visit with Kylen for the weekend. Alex answered the door in pajamas and a sweatshirt this evening. She had her hair cornrowed and even wore eyeglasses. She looked like the typical high school student. Seeing this look made me wonder how I missed the fact that she was a kid. All of those times that I saw Alex during my marriage to Jalen she was dressed so provocatively, that no one would have known that she was so young. If only I had taken a second to look deep into her eyes, I would have had a clue.

"Hey schoolgirl. Studying hard?" I asked as I walked into Alex's condo. "Girl yes. I have that math exam Monday, remember?" Alex immediately went back to her books on the couch and sat them in her lap. She began to turn the pages in the math book as the talked, "I quit school at fifteen. I tried to go back after I had Chris but I couldn't keep up so I quit. I am a little out of practice when it comes to math so I have to study harder than most people. But I am actually catching on okay. So what are you all getting into tonight?"

"I am taking them to eat pizza and to the movies tonight. Tomorrow we will probably stay in and rent a movie. We have church on Sunday and I will bring them back Sunday after dinner." I paused in hesitation before asking the next question. "Do you want to meet us at church?"

"Church? I ain't been to church in years. Sure I'll meet you there."

"I'm sure you know where it is. Since you did crash my wedding and all." I laughed as I made the last statement. Alex's cheeks began to flush with embarrassment. Her voice took on a high pitch when she replied, "Oh yeah, did I ever tell you how sorry I was about that?"

"Yeah you were sorry alright. And you had the nerve to wear white. Honey you were dead wrong."

"I know I was wrong, but tell the truth Mel, I was sharp wasn't I? That dress I had on was the bomb." Alex laughed and high-fived me, just before her expression grew solemn. "No really, I am truly sorry. I get embarrassed when I think about all of the mess that I did."

"Alex, it's okay now. That was the past. Besides, I probably would have done the same thing in your position. So do you have the boys' things packed? Kylen is waiting impatiently on us." Alex went to the bottom of the stairs and yelled, "Chris, Chase—get your stuff and come on. Miss Melany is here." They both came running noisily down the steps, Chase at a much slower pace than the bigger and stronger Chris. As we walked out the door I turned and looked at Alex, "Good luck with the studying."

"Yeah I sure need it, bye ya'll."

"Oh wait, can you walk outside with me Alex? There is something that I need to tell you." Alex and I walked outside to the SUV and each one of us strapped one of the boys down in the backseat. Once they were secure Alex looked at me and asked, "What's up?"

"I saw Jalen and Victor today."

"For real?" Alex's eyebrows were raised as she spoke. "Did he say anything to you?"

"No." I paused, and then continued, "He and Victor are together. I mean together-together. I saw them holding hands and kissing at this restaurant. All of the times that I thought Jalen was out with you, he was really seeing Victor. I owe you an apology. You told me that you didn't see my husband romantically during our marriage and I didn't believe you."

"Mel." Alex had a tear running as she spoke. "It's okay. I wouldn't have believed me either. I can't believe he's gay. I guess that's why he hasn't even tried to call and check on his kids. Look, I gotta get back to studying. Thanks for telling me about Jalen. I will see you Sunday."

Disappointment was written all over Alex's face. It was obvious that she was not completely over Jalen. I knew the pain that she was feeling, and I understood her wanting to be alone. I hugged Alex and quietly got into the SUV, as she walked slowly towards her front door. She dragged her feet with every step that she took. Once inside the truck, the high spirits of the children immediately uplifted me. After saying a quick prayer for Alex, I rode off into the sunset with my three favorite men.

Chapter 11

Business was very heavy and I stayed busy directing a few of my new workers on how to set the tables properly, prepare food, and deal with customers. "A Real Touch of Class" was already well-known throughout the city as ART-OC. We'd been in business for about two months and had already reclaimed all of the clients and customers that we surrendered to Jalen six months before. The décor was classy, the food was delicious and I tried to remain gracious as the owner. Kaiya took care of the Public Relations and sent a huge number of press releases out prior to the Grand Opening. We hosted hundreds of customers on our very first day of business and since that time we have maintained or exceeded it daily.

I was truly thankful for all of the blessings that God had sent my way. Alex was only weeks away from graduating from an accelerated diploma program and worked for me as a Manager during the evening shift. On numerous occasions, I was asked how I could be so kind to the mother of Jalen's illegitimate children. I constantly reminded others and myself that her kids are a blessing and well-behaved and that she was with Jalen before my marriage, though our timing overlapped slightly. Further more, I had seen blessings to an extent that no man could understand and therefore I felt obligated to be a blessing in others' lives.

I stood in the mirror putting the final touches on my hair as I anticipated what my day would entail. I had just gained approval for a home loan and was set to put an offer in today on a beautiful home that I found only miles away from ART-OC. It would be the first real purchase that I had ever made on my own in my life. Everything that I'd had in life up until now, had been given to me, or co-signed for by someone else. This home would belong to the kids and I, and this thought elated me.

As I shuffled through the house, quickly gathering my things, my phone began to ring. I expected it to be Kaiya because she was supposed to join me today. With a huge smile in my voice, I lifted the phone to my ear and greeted the caller, "This is Melany Starks."

"Melany this is Victor." An awkward silence controlled the moment as I searched for words to use. "Mel?"

"Yeah this is Mel. What is it Victor?"

"I am calling you for Jalen. He wanted me to tell you something. Jalen was diagnosed with terminal cancer around the time that you two separated. He didn't tell anyone about it because he hoped that they could cure him. Melany, it spread too quickly through his body. The doctors say that he only has a few weeks or so to live. He wants you and the kids to come over so he can say his good-byes. Just so you know, I won't be there if you do decide to come over. I moving back home so he can concentrate on you all. That is how he wants it."

"Victor, you don't have to leave what is obviously your new home with Jalen, because the kids and I won't be there that long—if at all." My voice was cold and hostile as I spoke to Victor. "If he is as sick as you say he is, I will bring Kylen, Victoria, and the boys over, but I won't allow them to stay too long. I don't think it would be healthy for them. They haven't seen his face in six months. So why start now? Victoria is now walking and trying to talk, he has already missed most of her life. But you can let him know that we may come by a little later."

"Mel, I understand that you are still upset but please understand that once Jalen is gone—he won't be able to come back. It will be too late and we don't get "do-overs" in real life. He needs to be around people that love him right now."

"Oh!" I yelled angrily in a high-pitched tone. "You mean like I needed to be around people I loved when I was giving birth to Victoria without him. Or how about when he ignored me in his speech at the banquet? Maybe we can discuss the trips he took with you, leaving me at home alone. Let's talk about how Alex will need years to make up for the time she lost from being sexually controlled by Jalen for so long. It was his choice to be away from his kids, he didn't even try to get them during the divorce or see them after the divorce. You know why? It was because he didn't care about seeing them then. Like I said, I will try to bring the kids to see him—but I can't make any promises beyond that."

"Okay Melany. Hope you can drop by. Good-bye."

"Yeah, bye Victor." I hung the phone up quickly. I couldn't let Victor hear the emotion that began to creep into my heart. Though, I had moved on from my relationship with Jalen, he was still my first love and the father of my children. He was an absolute jerk to me and an awful father to Kylen, Kaylen, Chris, and Chase after the divorce. However, I couldn't swallow the thought of him no longer being a part of this world—living and breathing.

My mind served as a scale balancing anger against sympathy, love against hatred, and revenge against forgiveness. The lines of what was expected of me in this situation began to blur. My kids were losing their father and they should have been the ones that counted. I began to pray for the strength to forgive Jalen and his treatment of us in the past. I prayed that God would guide me on the right things to do in this situation.

Once the prayer was over, it was clear in my mind what needed to be done. I would give my children the chance to get to know their father in a whole new light before he died. Hopefully, this would give them a wonderful memory of him and prevent any future breakdowns that they may feel about his death as they get older.

I held the phone impatiently as I waited on Kaiya to answer. "Hello!" I said anxiously as she answered the phone. I began to speak quickly, jumbling my words. "Ky, Jalen is really sick. He has cancer and is dying. Ky, I know you probably won't understand this, but I am going to take the kids over to spend a lot of time with him until he passes. Can you please watch over ART-OC for a few days?"

"What? Mel, you can't just call me and give me that much information all at one time. What do you mean Jalen is dying? He is so young."

"The doctors found cancer right after we split up and it spread quickly. Victor said that he only has a few weeks or so to live. I guess it runs in his family. I know that his mother wasn't the first person to die of cancer in his family. He told me that a few of his family members had cancer."

"Now Melany Lanae, don't you worry about what anyone else thinks. If you feel like you need to let your kids spend time with him—then you should do it. I think it's the right thing to do and it takes a big person to let go of the past and put their kids first. I will take care of everything at work. You just do what you have to do. Have you told Alex?"

When that question left Kaiya's lips, I shuddered at the thought of Alex's reaction to this news. Though Jalen had hurt her badly, and not spoken to her in eight months or so; she still held a big place for him in her heart. She remained strong in their separation but secretly awaited the day that she and he would reunite. I don't think she even fully understood or believed that Jalen was gay. In a solemn voice, I ended my call with Kaiya, and dialed Alex's number to give her some of the worst news that she would ever receive.

"Hey Mel." Alex answered the phone in a cheerful mood. "I got my cap and gown today. Can you believe it? I am really going to graduate." I tried to sound cheerful as Alex explained how she would be graduating with a high B average. Then just when I felt like I couldn't put it off any longer I interrupted her, "Alex, I got something to tell you."

"Okay. What's up?" I took a deep breath and paused before answering her. "Alex, Victor just called me. Jalen is dying of cancer…", a scream came across the line that caused the hair on the back of my neck to stand up. Alex came back to the phone and began to yell questions in my ear, "What do you mean dying? Maybe he was joking."

"Alex, he wouldn't joke about something like that."

"Who told him that? Why didn't he call me? What happened? What am I going to do? What about the kids? Mel, I can't raise these boys by myself."

"Alex, you have been raising the boys without Jalen for their whole lives. You are a good mother. Don't worry about that. You just pray and ask God to help you with them. Jalen wanted me to bring them over to visit with him. Is it okay if I come get them sometime?"

"When can I see him Melany?" Alex was still very hysterical as if Jalen was already dead. "Didn't he want to see me?"

"Victor called me." I answered her calmly. "I am not sure about that. I will ask him when I get there with the kids. Alex this is not about you or me—this is about Jalen getting to be with his kids before he dies. Try to remember that he is no longer involved with either of us, he is only the father of our kids."

"Okay, I get it. You can come get them later. Is there anything you need me to do?" Alex was talking in between sobs as she tried to gain her composure. "I need you to watch over things at the restaurant okay?" I spoke slowly to Alex, in an effort to ensure that she was hearing me. "Now is the time to step up for your kids, Alex. I will talk to you about everything later."

The ride to Jalen's house was absolutely silent. I thought about the comments that I would hear from most of the people I knew. "How can you take care of someone who treated you so bad? Girl I wouldn't do a thing for him after the way he did you." I began to ask why I was on my way to visit this demon from my past. But no matter how I worded the questions, the answer always came back to my kids. I wanted them to feel like they knew their Dad in a special way. I didn't want him to leave this earth without telling them just how much he loves them. This would not only be the last days of Jalen's life—it would be the last of their father's life too. So no one else's opinion mattered— my kids were the reason that I would sacrifice my own comfort.

I pulled into the driveway and began to feel a familiar anxiety growing in my chest. It was the exact same anxiety that I would feel on the days that I came home and Jalen wasn't there. I slowly put the car in park at the end of the driveway. This is where visitors would park when I lived there. The area that used to serve as my parking space was open and available however, I did not park there. I left it open as a symbolic testament to Jalen's place in my life. I was now only a guest at his home.

I got out of the car and walked up to Jalen's door, fumbling with my keys. Before I could even knock, Jalen cracked the door and peaked out at me. Once he saw that it was me—he slowly opened the door wider. Initially his appearance startled me. He stood there me in a silk bathrobe and pajamas. He looked as if he had lost about 60 pounds and his face was splotchy. Jalen's hair was unkempt and his skin was very dry and somewhat scaly. I smiled nervously at him, trying desperately not to stare at his changing face. "Hey Jalen, I heard you were under the weather; so I brought you some visitors. They are sure to cheer you up."

"Where are they?" Jalen looked around with a big smile on his face as he spoke. "Don't just stand out there come on in." I turned and began to jog to the car to get the kids. Kylen had awakened from his road nap and was already calling out to his father in excitement. Victoria woke up, startled by Kylen's sudden yelling and laughter. I unbuckled Kylen from his seat and he ran up to the doorway where Jalen was standing with open arms. Slowly I removed Victoria from her seat and began to walk towards the big white house. When I was only steps away from Jalen, he shifted his eyes to Victoria and stared at her for seconds. She was only a small baby when he saw her last and she had since stretched out into a long legged little girl with curly pigtails and pretty brown eyes. Jalen put Kylen down, gave him a pat on the butt, and told him to run inside; then slowly extended his arms to hold Kaylen.

As I transferred her into Jalen's arms; my eyes began to water. Jalen looked like a skeleton of himself. His eyes were sunken in and dark but they were still very deep and familiar. His hands were thin but his touch was still very strong. I realized then that it was not the cancer that made me unable to see the Jalen that I married; it was the fact that he was no longer the man that I knew. It was as if I was meeting him for the very first time. Jalen held the sleepy Victoria in his arms as he stared at her face. She reached out and grabbed his lips and pulled both of them creating a duck bill affect. Her playfulness caused Jalen and me to laugh, breaking the ice. Jalen looked over at me, smiled and led me into his home. "Come on in. I am so glad that you came by. Are you all hungry?"

"Daddy I am. I want pizza." Kylen answered as he ran up to his old room. Jalen followed Kylen up the steps with Kaylen in his arms. He moved slowly but still tried to hide his true pain. "Mel." Jalen yelled back down the steps to me. "Could you order pizza?"

"Yeah. I'll order it." I walked into the kitchen to use the phone. As I walked through the house, I tried to picture myself there and was unable to. The memories of this home were now so distant that I had a hard time picturing my life here. I reached out and picked up the wall phone in the kitchen. As I dialed, I looked around at the few changes that had been made. Jalen had bought a new wine rack, new stove, and a new refrigerator. The sleek new refrigerator had a picture of Victor and Jalen on it dated the day before Kaylen's birth. They were standing together romantically on what appeared to be a beach. Pictures of Kylen and Victoria were also posted on the refrigerator in cute little frames that said "Daddy's little girl" for her and "Daddy's helper" for Kylen. I quickly looked away and began to dial the number to the pizzeria. I ordered Jalen's favorite pizza and one of Kylen's favorites and then quietly went back to the living room.

I was sitting with both feet crossed under me in a lazy boy thumbing through a magazine when Jalen and the kids came back down stairs. Jalen plopped down on the couch and began to tickle Kylen before saying, "Kylen, your Daddy is tired. Let me rest for a minute." Jalen looked over at me and said, "I never used to get tired. Now I get tired from walking to the living room." After a short pause he continued, "Melany, what made you come. I mean, after all the things that I have done to you. Why would you even care enough to come by?"

"Jalen this isn't about you or me; it's about them." I said as I pointed to our children. "They deserve to have a relationship with their father even if I don't want a relationship with their father. Even if their father cancels their insurance; they still deserve to know both parents. So I decided to look over your actions and do the right thing."

"Well, Melany. You are right. I don't deserve it but I am glad that you decided to bring them. I don't know if Victor told you the whole story but—I feel the need to explain. I have always thought that I was gay, Mel. I just didn't know how to face it; I didn't want to be that way. So I did everything that I could to try to convince myself that I wasn't. I knew that I loved Victor when I was 18 years old; but he and I refused to face it. So for years I acted like I was a player. I slept with all kinds of women to prove that I was straight. That's where that stuff with Alex happened. I was just out of residency and not thinking clearly. I didn't like what was happening between her and me, but I couldn't risk her telling anyone. I would have lost everything. I know I was wrong and I made a lot of mistakes Mel. I shouldn't have pulled you into it because you didn't ask for that type of life. I am sorry. I hope that one day you can forgive me. Even if it's long after I'm gone; I hope one day you will forgive me."

"Jalen, let's not talk about that." I quickly changed the subject because I did not want to give in to his apologies and become overly sympathetic for him. "So what is the doctor saying about your health?"

"Mel. I only have a few weeks to live. They say that any day now, my body will stop being able to handle its daily functions and then from there, things will slowly end. The cancer started in my stomach and has made its way through my whole body. Considering that I am a doctor, I can tell that it won't be long for me. I have some okay days but the majority of them are painful and depressing." By this time Jalen was tearful. He was not bawling and he spoke calmly and carefully with consideration to the kids as the tears fell quietly. "I never thought that I would die this early. I spend my days healing people and now that I need healing, there's no chance. I guess I deserve it."

"Jalen, this is not happening because you deserve it. God has a plan for each of us. This is happening to you for a reason; it's up to you to figure out that reason and fulfill it in time. I tell you what; wipe those tears before you bum the kids out and enjoy the party." Jalen looked up at me in bewilderment and asked, "What party?"

"…The party that we are going to have for the next few days. I brought the kids and clothes; they are going to stay with you and party all day and night." As I said this I walked over to the CD player and put on music. Kylen jumped up and grabbed his father by the hand and bounced around in a dancing manner. With Kaylen in my arms, I danced around the room. As I danced, I felt sorry for Jalen yet I had become a master at hiding my real feelings.

The doorbell rang about one minute into the dancing and I volunteered to answer the door. I put Kaylen down on the floor and danced my way to the front door. After paying for the pizza, I closed the door quickly as the delivery man walked back to his car. Pizza in hand, I stood in the foyer of the house and began to fight the tears that welled up in my eyes. No longer was I in love with Jalen; but never did I want to see him in this shape. I guess that I was secretly hoping that once I got here, I would see that Victor was joking, or maybe over-exaggerating the seriousness of the situation. It was one thing to raise my kids "alone for the most part" but to raise them "completely alone" was another thing that I had not prepared myself for. Only seconds later, I heard the pitter-patter of little feet. Kylen ran up to me full of excitement and said, "Mama c'mon. I wanna eat." I wiped my tears, took a deep breath and said "I'm coming. Go on back in there with Daddy."

We ate pizza and watched a movie as a family for the first time in months, a year maybe. I sat on the couch while Jalen and the kids all laid on the floor. His nurse stopped in to make sure that he had his medicine and to check up on things. Kylen began to ask questions while she checked his vitals and Jalen answered them calmly and truthfully. "Daddy is sick Kylen. This nice lady takes care of me." Kylen was obviously satisfied with that answer and went right back to watching the movie.

After falling asleep on the movie, I was awakened to the noise of Jalen tidying up the room. The kids were not in sight so I slowly sat up. "Where are the kids?"

"I put them to bed. It's almost ten."

"Okay. I am going to go on home…"

"Mel, please don't go home. I made the guestroom up for you and put your stuff in there. I am not trying to sweet talk you or anything. I just want the kids to have a normal family experience before I go. Please Mel, can we all stay under one roof just for now?" Jalen looked me in the eyes as he spoke. He rarely did this during our marriage. There was desperation on his face; for once he seemed sincere. I reached out and touched Jalen's hand as I walked past him. "I'll see you in the morning. We are all going out for pancakes. So you better get some rest."

"Pancakes it is!" Jalen breathed a sigh of relief as I walked into the downstairs guestroom and closed the door behind me. Once inside I laid on the bed and began to write in my journal. I tried to put my feelings on paper as a release. No one including myself could understand why I was here putting myself through this trauma. I would write my feelings every night hoping that one day—I could read it and truly understand why I was there.

The weeks up until then with Jalen were full of ups and downs. We never mentioned our relationship and spent almost all of our time discussing the kids and what to do after he passed. Jalen was declining quickly and had spent the last few days in the bed unable to gain the strength to move around. When Chris and Chase weren't there, Kylen would do puzzles with Jalen, while Victoria sat in Jalen's lap and smiled. I took picture after picture of them all, carefully capturing moments for the kids to cherish later.

Jalen's doctor brought bad news to him on a Wednesday. Jalen's body was now starting to shutdown. While there was no way of knowing when he would die—it was safe to say that he would not be in this world much longer. I watched as Jalen coughed madly and ached from the smallest touch. Before long, he was unable to allow Kylen to sit in the bed with him due to the pain.

Nearly three weeks into our visit, I was in the kitchen preparing lunch for Jalen and the kids when the door bell rang. I walked to the door as I wiped my hands on my apron. Assuming it was the nurse, I answered the door without asking who it was. Victor stood there, looking noticeably thinner and depressed. He wore dress slacks, a slightly wrinkled dress shirt that looked like yesterday, and no tie. He had his briefcase in his right hand and a shopping bag in his left. "Hey Mel. I came to take care of Jalen's final wishes and will. Oh and I brought these for the kids." Victor handed me the bag and slowly stepped inside the house. I peaked in the bag. It contained new toys and clothes for both Kylen and Kaylen. The t-shirt that was on the top was pink and read "My Daddy Loves Me."

Victor never looked at me in the eyes and kicked at imaginary dirt on the floor. He was far from the arrogant attorney that was at the mediation hearing. Realizing that Victor was uncomfortable with facing me for the first time since the restaurant, I reached out and hugged him. We were both losing someone important to us and I had forgiven them both for everything. "Come on in. Jalen is in his room. Are you hungry?"

"Now Melany, you know I am always hungry. By the way, congratulations on your business. I heard it is blowing up."

"Yeah thanks. It is doing pretty well. Jalen, Victor is here." I waited for Jalen to respond and opened the door after he did. Never looking to see how Jalen would react; I let Victor in and quietly closed the door behind me, leaving them alone. I then went upstairs and took the kids their gifts.

Within minutes, Victor called me back into the room where he and Jalen were. I walked into the room, feeling slightly uncomfortable from the idea of sharing space with my ex-husband and his lover. "Mel, come on in and sit down." Jalen was speaking to me in a near whisper. Jalen waited a moment for me to take a seat and began to speak. "I want you to take care of everything when I am gone. I have arranged for you to get just about everything when I die. This house is paid for and will go to you and all of my kids. Please see to it that Alex gets what she needs for the boys. I have taken care of them all in the will but if she needs anything else, I want you to take care of it. Victor is going to make sure that you get the restaurant back and that everything isn't tied up in litigation. I have given him a safety deposit box that is to be opened by you only after I pass. Mel, I would like for Victor to get this box that I am giving you after I die. The money, cars, practice, and everything will go to you Melany. I have two new doctors already working there; I only need you to take care of the business side of it. I would like for it to remain in the family, but if gets to be too much and you must sell it at any point in time—I understand. Most of all, I want you both to know that I am so sorry for hurting you. Melany you were a wonderful wife and I thank you for giving me such beautiful kids. Victor, you waited on me for years and I just led you on. I am sorry. You are a great friend and I love you." Jalen's whisper had turned into a quiet sob. His emaciated frame quaked as he reached out and touched my face. "Please take care of my babies. I know you have to go on with your life but please Mel, don't let them forget me. I screwed up your life and some of theirs and I am so sorry. Just make sure they know that their Daddy wasn't perfect but he loved them and their mother more than life itself."

"I will Ja…" the moment became too much for me and I too began to cry—unable to finish my sentence. I watched as Victor's shoulders dropped and he put his face into his hands. The paperwork that he had in his lap was covered in tear drops. Slowly, I stood up and walked out of the room. The four walls were suffocating me. My emotions wrapped around my neck and were squeezing the life from my body. Once outside of the room and safely in the guestroom, I retreated under the blankets of my bed, peaking out only to see if the sunshine of a new day was visible.

I woke up the following morning feeling a sense of obligation to Jalen and to God. I was well aware of the fact that Jalen and I did not speak of salvation as a family, which made it more likely than not that he was unsure of his salvation as an individual. I went into Jalen's room prepared to speak with him about his soul. When I entered the room, Jalen was lying perfectly still, with his eyes open. "Jalen?" I whispered so as not to startle him. He slowly looked over at me and answered, "Huh Mel?"

"Can I talk to you for a minute?" I walked in and sat on the bed next to Jalen. "Jalen do you think you will go to heaven when you die?" Jalen looked at me, surprised at the question. I continued to talk. "I don't want to be a bother, but I think this is something that we need to talk about."

"Yeah Mel, we probably should talk about it. I don't know whether I will go to heaven or not. I know that I believe in God and I know that I haven't exactly lived according to his word. If God is truly keeping score, then I probably won't make it to heaven." It pained my heart to listen to Jalen speak that way, however I appreciated his honesty. "Jalen, you have to go to him and earnestly repent. He wants to welcome you and forgive you—all you have to do is ask. First you speak to him, then you work on forming a personal relationship with him."

"Don't you think it's a little late for that Mel? I am about half dead now. I have lived my life for the moment and ignored him for this long. God will probably ignore me now that I need him."

"Jalen if you ask for forgiveness, he can wipe your slate clean. It would be like nothing else matters but that moment. Just think about it Jalen. I will be praying for you." Jalen shook his head in agreement and bowed his head slowly.

The following day death loomed in the air and I knew that Jalen would be gone before long. I called the nurse for Jalen and informed her of his condition. She came quickly and checked his vitals before assuring me that he would probably live, at least for the next few days. Later in the evening, Jalen's pain intensified and he became almost unresponsive. In the midst of being there for Jalen, I hadn't taken the time to take care of myself. My hair was in a messy ponytail and my clothes were fitting noticeably bigger as I entered into his bedroom and sat by his bedside, rubbing his head.

I tried to take in every detail of his face, and the fear that it held. He wore no expression whatsoever; however his eyes, sat deep inside his face, were telling me everything he was feeling. I let Kylen and Kaylen see him before bed and even for them he said nothing. Now, while our angels slumbered soundly, I sat by Jalen's bedside trying to comfort him. Over the past few weeks that I was with Jalen he and I became friends. Now as I looked at his small tired frame, I began to remember the man that he was. I pictured him standing in front of me laughing: tall, dark and gorgeous. I pictured him picking me up and spinning me around after I told him that I was pregnant with Kylen. I pictured him holding both Kylen and Kaylen for the first time. That was the man that I would remember and celebrate.

Once Jalen's breathing became even and quiet, I knew that he had fallen asleep. I kissed him on his cheek, adjusted the cover and went to my room for the night. That night, I wrote about Jalen and the good times only. I placed all of the bad memories in a vault and locked them away for good. I had forgiven him and hopefully God had too. I wrote for hours about my first love, the father of my children, and my new friend.

The morning sun crept quietly into my bedroom waking me. I wore the same clothes from the night before and had fallen asleep on my journal. The skin stood eerily up on the back of my neck as I rolled over and out of bed. I went to the kids' rooms to check on them and they were sleeping peacefully. The clock read 6:15am as I made the way into Jalen's room to say good-morning and to give him his meds. I opened the door and peeked in to keep from disturbing him if he wasn't already awake.

Jalen was lying there in a permanent state of peace. I reached out and touched his face, knowing full well that it would be cold. His eyes were closed and his dark lips were turned up slightly. My heart began to pound in my chest with every second of realization.

Jalen left us sometime during the night and only his body remained this morning. I shook him violently, hoping that he would perhaps open one eye and say good-bye. He didn't. I held his hand in mine as I dropped my head in tearful prayer. I had spent weeks preparing for this and still I wasn't prepared.

Slowly, I raised my head and looked at Jalen one more hard time, sharing this moment alone with him. His pale skin was now peaceful and he wore his wedding band on a necklace around his neck. I had been wearing my beautiful diamond band on my right hand. I took it off and placed it too on the necklace that Jalen wore and put it away safely. I kissed my friend softly on his cheek before quietly leaving the room.

Kaiya came and picked up the kids while I waited on the ambulance and coroner to come and get Jalen. As they pulled off with Kaiya, Kylen looked around for his father. I smiled and waved at him hoping that I would be enough to comfort him. In my heart I began to hope that I would be enough for both Kylen and Kaylen; Jalen was gone and I had no one but God to help me raise them.

I followed all of Jalen's wishes in planning his homegoing celebration. His funeral had about 1000 people in attendance, and was well publicized. To many, Jalen was a young, black, successful doctor and entrepreneur. He was a Man of the Year honoree and well liked within the community. To me, he was a friend and the father of my children, so I said good-bye in my own special way. I did not sit with Jalen's family at the funeral. I did not want the focus to be on me or our marriage. It was Jalen's last day to shine.

There were many tears shed for him, many kind words said about him and many donations made in his honor. A popular florist in the area supplied one free rose to every person who attended his burial. By the time everyone had placed their flowers down on his grave, Jalen's plot was covered and the beauty leaked over onto neighboring plots. As the dirt was placed on Jalen's casket, his memory moved into the hearts of many including his children and me.

I didn't return to our home until about a week after Jalen's funeral. I left Kylen and Victoria with Alex, and went to prepare the home for our move. As I pulled into the driveway, I was immediately touched by the gifts and flowers that had been placed on the doorstep by the neighbors. There were gift baskets, teddy bears, flowers, and a wreath decorated with ribbon. I slowly picked each item up and brought them all in the house.

My heart first led me to Jalen's room. There were no sheets on the bed and all of Jalen's medicine was still on the nightstand. I began to place each bottle in a box, when I noticed the deposit box sitting on the floor at the foot of the bed. A note on the box had, "To my favorite girl" written in Jalen's perfect handwriting. I picked it up and sat on the bed with the box in my lap. I was unable to open it yet. Opening it would mean that Jalen was gone for good. By saving this, I still would have one more surprise from him. I ran my hand over the note and sat the box down gently before going back to work on the room.

I put all of his medicine away, put his clothes carefully away in boxes, and put the pictures I'd taken of him in a scrapbook. After about 9 hours of work, the house was ready for the kids and me to move into. It was full of memories of Jalen; however it had all the qualities of home. After I finished, I had a seat on the couch and looked through the scrapbook of Jalen and the kids. In my lap, I held the security box that Jalen had sat aside for me. Tears ran down my face as I tried to coach myself into opening it. Jalen said to only open it after he died. My hands shook as I rung my hands together thoughtfully. I held a conversation with myself in my mind, "Mel, if you open this box, it will mean that Jalen is gone forever. Are you able to cope with this?" I nodded my head in response to my conversation with my inner-self. Slowly, I opened the case and peered through its contents. A huge smile slowly crept across my face as I picked up each item in the box: the bill from our first date, the program from my college commencement, his menu selection form from the first time I catered one of his affairs, the nasty dipsticks from each one of my pregnancies, a negative HIV test dated only weeks before his death, and a letter written in Jalen's nice handwriting. Each item was crucially important parts of our lives together and by holding on to these—Jalen showed me that he did care for me in some way. Maybe it wasn't in the way that a wife would hope for her husband to care, however I could now rest a little better, knowing that he cherished the special moments just as much as I did. I placed each item back in the box, but kept only the letter out. Slowly, I closed the box and placed it on the floor. Then, I stood to my feet and walked out onto the patio.

I sat on the patio with my feet up on the patio table in front of me and opened the letter slowly. As I read it—I cried, as I cried—I healed, and as I healed, I thanked God for the revelation that he finally sent to me in Jalen's own voice. The letter explained why he was the man that he was, it told his story, the real story that he was unable to mumble to anyone. Jalen was speaking to me and confiding in me the things that he could tell no one else in life. After the letter was over, I stood up and placed it safely in my pocket. I walked to the edge of the patio and set on the rail. The pool sparkled clear, blue, and peaceful from one end of my backyard to the other. Thoughts of

Jalen flooded my mind as I pondered on how he decided to spend the last days of his life.

Jalen's last days with Kylen, Kaylen, Chris and Chase were full of happy times. Finally, I understood why I agreed to come and be with Jalen until his passing. It gave me a chance to finally get to know the man that I took as my husband. But most importantly, it gave us all time to mend some of the broken relationships.

Chapter 12

▼

While it did take some time to get used to living in the house once shared with Jalen, and the same house where he passed; the kids and I were able to comfortably call it home only a few months after the funeral. In the weeks that followed Jalen's passing, I wrote in my journal daily as a way of recording my victories. These victories were not the kind that left opponents as losers. They were the kind of victories that left everyone in a better state and no one compromised. I spoke with people daily who knew Jalen or had caught wind of the situation between him and me. Many of them questioned every single thing I did that was forgiving and praised all of the vengeful things I did. However, every time I was asked about my life and the choices I made; I used it as a window opened up for the purpose of sharing some of the lessons I learned.

Now, approximately one year after Jalen's death, I stood backstage of a "Women on the Move" Convention, nervously looking through my cue cards. This was the second appearance that I had made as a speaker and I was still nervous about what would come out of my mouth. The emcee was onstage speaking about me as she prepared to introduce me to the crowd. As she named off my accomplishments and credentials; I began to feel more and more humbled. It was as if the lady that she was describing was a powerful strong woman, with awesome intelligence and sharp wit. Here I stood, a mess in nice clothes, with no sense of self-direction; my every move was guided by God. I felt honored to share my life with others. It was by no fault of my own that I was brought from a life of constant tears and pain. What did I have to share and who would want to listen to me? As she called my name and I began to walk out on the stage, I felt that familiar spiritual tap on the shoulder. Instantly, I was relaxed, reassured, and ready to affect change.

I stepped up to the podium, looked around at the audience in acknowledgement and appreciation and began to tell my story. I told every detail and watched as the audience gave the looks of utter disgust at how ignorant I had been. I told of the hurt and watched as eyes became teary. Finally I told of the forgiveness and watched as some became perplexed. When I'd finished with telling the story of my life, I looked at the crowd and put away my cue cards, allowing myself to speak from the heart.

"While I know many of you listened to my story and heard nothing but the bad times; I wish that at least some of you could step back and look deeply for the lesson in it. Trouble comes sometimes in a big way but God always has something special on the horizon for his children. Forgiveness is not ignorance; it's necessary. It lightens the load on your shoulders and touches the hearts of those who have wronged you.

I could sit here and tell you all that I am completely over everything that has happened to me in my life. I could stand here and act as if, I walked through life completely unfazed by what others thought of me, or my life. The truth is—the things that I shared here with you tore me into pieces. Yes, my husband dogged me, yes I lost everything that I had, and yes I had no family but my kids to be there with me through it all. To tell the truth…," I paused as the power of the words began to move me to tears. "I should have been dead and gone. I was so close to killing my self, when God stepped in and made the difference. He touched my heart and reminded me of just how much he loves Melany. I gave it all to him and he slowly began to work things out for me.

I began to pray for myself and for others. I prayed for people I loved, people I disliked and even people I didn't know so well. I have now been able to step back and watch in disbelief as blessings unfold. Young ladies, I watched as Alex became strong and focused and her kids became "our" kids. I watched as the Lord replaced my mother's business that was taken from me with a new legacy that is thriving now. Most importantly, I learned to forgive and I watched as a dying man undid many of the mistakes he made in life, allowing him to die in peace.

My children are now able to have meaningful relationships with their brothers that will last their whole lives. I too have developed a new friend in a very unlikely place, the mother of my ex-husband's children. Going through those storms reinforced and strengthened my relationship with my very best friend.

So, if you are able to be a blessing in someone's life through forgiveness, please do so. You never know when your life will intertwine with another's and create something meaningful or magical. In closing, I would like to thank Kaiya and each and every one of you who held on to me in my time of need. Thank you for your time and may God bless you all."

I watched as the crowd slowly rose to its feet in ovation. In the crowd I saw several familiar faces all of which were emotionally touched by seeing me use my life to try to reach out to others. Quietly and humbly I exited the stage and began the short walk to my dressing area. I sat at the vanity and stared at the woman in the mirror, thankful for what she had become. There was a light tapping on the door and in walked Kaiya with Kylen, Kaylen, Alex, Chase, and Chris. Each one of the kids hugged me and handed me a single rose, while both Alex and Kaiya were clearly too emotional to say much of anything.

After spending time with my family and receiving some of the people from the audience, I gathered my things and began to make my way to the car. My arms became full rather quickly with the many extra suits that I brought "just in case". I juggled the items in my arms while I walked to my car, through the dimly lit parking lot. Out of nowhere, appeared Victor and another man in the shadows that I couldn't see very well. "Ms. Starks, can I assist you?"

"No I'm fine. Victor is that you?" I kissed him on the cheek quickly and smiled as I spoke to him. "Boy, what are you doing here?"

"I caught word that there was going to be an awesome speaker here tonight and I just had to come and hear her for myself." He too smiled as he spoke to me, "And believe me she was definitely awesome. Oh excuse my manners. This is my friend, Anton. Anton this is…"

"Honey, I already know Melany Starks." Anton stepped out of the shadows and gave me a hug. "Girl I haven't seen you since I left Kaiya's shop."

"Hey Anton." I spoke trying to hide my surprise as I figured out just how deep the pool of deception had been. "So Victor was the Tory you were talking about all of those times in the shop. I never would have guessed it. Anyway, we miss you at the shop. How is your shop doing?"

"Girl, it's doing okay. I am still tying to build clientele, but you know how that is. But you know me, I'm gone do what I do regardless." Anton was about to keep up the conversation when Victor stopped him with obvious embarrassment and said, "I see you two have met. Mel, I put everything in your car for you. We gotta run. I just wanted to stop by and congratulate you on a wonderful speech. Oh and thanks for not using my name in the story. I'm out of the closet but not that far out." Victor followed that statement with nervous laughter as he prepared to walk away. We all exchanged quick good-byes and I watched in disbelief as Victor and Anton left hand in hand.

While I should have suspected such, Victor had played Jalen all along. Anton was in Victor's life while I was married to Jalen and even Jalen's death didn't snap Victor out of this web of deceit that he was spinning. Seeing this in Victor made me even more relieved about Jalen's state when he passed. While no one can say for sure, it seemed apparent that he had repented and made his peace before it was too late.

I sat in my car thinking before I drove away. I thought about how things in the world are never as they seem initially, but in hindsight things are usually exactly as they seem. My thoughts were then interrupted by my cell phone. It was Kaiya calling. She and Alex were taking the kids out for a late dinner and wanted me to come along so we could celebrate my big night. I opened my mouth to accept her invitation but quickly changed my mind and agreed to just meet them a little later. There was one more stop that I needed to make.

I drove the car relying solely on fate as I nervously tapped the steering wheel with my thumbs. After about twenty minutes, I reached the parking lot that was the stage for some of the most dramatic moments in my life. This was the place where Jalen and I built his practice. It was where I found out that both of my kids were coming. This was the exact spot where Alex and I had our first real run-in. It had been here that I decided to end my life, and now it served as the spot where a sign stood in memory of Jalen's life.

The irony of the thoughts caused chills to run down my spine and tears to well in my eyes. I thought about the cold darkness that existed the evening that I contemplated suicide and realized that it was completely opposite of the warm star-filled night sky that I was sitting under. Slowly, I climbed out of my car and walked around to its hood. I slid my butt carefully up on the warm hood, removed each one of the heels that I was wearing and held them in my hands. I stared at Jalen's name and began to reflect on where I'd been and the journey that was ahead. From where I sat, things were looking up for my family, Kaiya, Alex, her family, and me. However, things still seemed to be spinning out of control for Victor now that Jalen was only a memory. Over a year ago, I wanted to give up on life, yet I was able to walk away and be a comfort to someone else as they lost their life. I spent most of my adult years searching for a replacement for my mother, and was now the only mother-figure that Alex knew.

A spiritual mentor of mine once told me that the darkest part of the night, is just before the break of day. For me the darkness had passed and I was living in a brand new day. Though it was evening outside; for me, my spirituality, my family, and my life the sun was just rising. Slowly, I slid off of the hood of my car, stretched, slid my feet into my heels, adjusted my skirt, and smiled; I was revived by the new day. I took one last look around and glanced again at Jalen's name before I pulled my car out of the parking space and drove off to meet my family. As I rode, I smiled in thankfulness for the lessons in life that had been revealed to me over time. I was now stronger in God and purposeful in my passion. Hopefully, my life would be a long drive for which the darkest mile had passed. Whatever the case, I was now equipped for anything, thankful for everything, and hiding from nothing.

Jalen's Last Words

Dear Mel,

As I sit here and write to you, cancer is taking away the very life that tried to ruin your life. While I may be too late with this apology to change the affect that my actions may have on you and our children, I hope that I am not too late to empower you and provide you with a little insight on the real Jalen Starks.

The truth is, I have always loved you. You are beautiful, strong, loyal, and kind. The day I married you, I felt so lucky to be the man that you chose to spend forever with. Only, I wasn't the man that you thought I was and loving you just wasn't enough to defeat the demons that lived inside of me. As a child, a few things were taken from me and what was left was not enough to help me to realize and walk in my true identity. I fell in love with Victor long before I met you and yes, I loved him too on the day that I married you. So while I was joyful for marrying you, it pained me to know that I was hurting Victor, my first love, and would eventually hurt you, my wife. I will not further your pain with the shameful details of my indiscretions; however I will say—it had very little to do with you Melany I was always the problem.

I will admit that I do owe you an explanation for my actions with Alex. It was grossly inappropriate and even today as I am dying—I regret the pain that I caused her. She was a young girl when I met her and she held so much pain in her eyes. It was the same pain that I felt as I fought with my identity and believe it or not—I felt like she and I could relate to one another. Her mother didn't care about her, and mine knew of the pain I experienced in my childhood and did nothing to shelter me from it. It felt good to be around her and for the moments that we were together—it didn't matter whether I was gay, bi-sexual, or straight. All that mattered was that she and I connected. Yes, somewhere along the way—it did click in my mind that this provocative, young lady was in fact just a little girl and I too was just as guilty as the person who invaded me. By that time Melany, it was too late and she was in the position to blackmail me into giving her everything that she needed to live a comfortable bill-free, motherless life. I am not saying that I didn't deserve it—I am only saying that I never meant for it to go that far.

There were so many times that I wanted to share my truth with you, but losing you would have been one more blow to my already aching ego. I felt as if my manhood was on the line and you held it all in your hand. As a man, I was supposed to have a wife, kids, and a successful career—and if I could manage all of these things—I thought that my sexuality wouldn't matter. Well, I was wrong and I failed the test of being a man.

I was a selfish father, an awful husband, and a pedophile—this I can now admit. Melany, while you owe me absolutely no favors, I ask that you find it in your heart to forgive me. I truly do love you and even now as I am dying you remain the best thing that ever happened to my life—short of Christ that is. Baby, kiss my kids on the nights that they miss me, hold them when the pain gets intense, and as they grow up please let them know that though their father made many mistakes, all four of them were blessings from heaven.

These are not just words on paper, Melany. This is what truly lies in my heart. And as the breath in my body diminishes, please know that it was your introduction of Christ into my life that made the difference. I am in constant communication with him and I have faith that eventually, even after my death, he will ease the hearts of you, Alex, and my babies. Melany, thank you so much and God bless.

P.S. Every time you think of me—kiss my kids. Please, take care of Alex—she really needs you. I love ya'll!

Love always,

Jalen
April, 05

Dear Misery,

So many years have passed since you've come into my life. As I prepare myself to become one with a woman who I don't deserve I feel that it's only fair that I expose you and the pain you've caused me since the first time you used my favorite uncle to introduce you to me. This is a letter written only in the event that I would gain enough strength to share the reason for my inner deep dark pain.

One mid summer evening after a family cook out, things were winding down for the family, and building up for me. My innocence was taken in a painful and inhumane way in a graphic and all too real depiction of how cruel life can be. I remember the smell, the blood, the alcohol on his breath and the tight grip he had around my neck. No one heard my screams and no one tended to my wounds. My manhood was shaken and my childhood was snatched. The pain still lives there and even now as I am about to take a beautiful woman as my wife—I am battling it. Misery, you have taken from me long enough. You have eaten away at my pride and bruised my self-esteem. I remain torn, between the man I am supposed to be and the man that I am.

As a teenager, I walked around from day-to-day in a haze of confusion. There was no group specific group that I could fit into; I was merely a follower of anyone who treated me as if I counted. I buried my pain in my schoolwork and used accomplishment to hide all of the pain that I held. I can still remember the day that the most popular guy in school said hello to me. It was Victor, and immediately he befriended me, taking me under his wing and helping me in my transition from silent and withdrawn, to dashing and debonair. Never again did I experience issues with women—I truly had my fair share, but no relationship compared to the one I shared with Victor. Together we did it all, played sports, played girls too old and too young, and even experimented with one another. There were no regrets after my first experience with Victor, no awkwardness—only real sincere emotions.

I still remember the day I met my lovely Melany. She was different—virginal and angelic. I wanted greatly to shed the layers of dirt that covered my lifestyle, just to make a simple commitment to this woman that could change my whole life. I was willing to deny my illegitimate children and their mother, push Victor away, and even conceal my real identity to keep this woman in my life.

Victor is still the only person who knows my secrets and even he refuses to allow me to live my life without outside input. The man who hurt me as a child, somehow still controls my life unknowingly. The woman who gave birth to me, also controls my life, the man that I love controls my life, and misery—you too control my life. I am at the point where I must take control and do what I as a man am supposed to do.

Today, I will evict you from my heart and walk into a life with Melany. I will say "I do" to the woman of my dreams while the man of my life stands by. Today is the day that you, misery, become a thing of the past.

Jalen
1999

978-0-595-40438-4
0-595-40438-3

Printed in the United States
88930LV00002B/340-372/A